The Midland Kid

TALES OF THE PRESIDENTIAL GHOSTWRITER

A novel of politics, petroleum, and poetry,
legacy and lunacy, the Middle East and the Old West

ALLAN APPEL

NEW HAVEN INDEPENDENT PRESS • NEW HAVEN, CONNECTICUT

IT'S YOUR TOWN. READ ALL ABOUT IT.

ISBN 978-1-4196-8883-6
Copyright © 2008 Allan Appel
Cover and book design by Sophie Appel
New Haven Independent Press books are published
by the New Haven Independent, c/o:

Online Journalism Project
P.O. Box 3288
Westville Station
New Haven, CT 06515

To order, visit *Amazon.com*
For information on author events, contact
editor@newhavenindependent.org

Profound thanks to my daughter Sophie Appel, Stuart Kramer, Forrest Stone, Paul Bass, Melissa Bailey, and The New Haven Independent *team for their enthusiasm, support, and good cheer. We're all hoping George W. Bush reads this novel, but we're not holding our breath.*

PREVIOUS BOOKS BY ALLAN APPEL

FICTION

The Rabbi of Casino Boulevard
Vengeance Valley
Judah
High Holiday Sutra
Club Revelation

NONFICTION

A Portable Apocalypse: A Quotable Companion to the End of the World
The Squire of East Hampton
To Life: 36 Stories of Memory and Hope

POETRY

New Listings
Not So Much Love of Flowers

Due to the lack of experienced trumpeters, the End of the World has been postponed for three weeks!
—SIGN HUNG ON THE CHAMBER OF THE RULES COMMITTEE,
U.S. HOUSE OF REPRESENTATIVES, 1970

One

Brewster George, President of the United States, was hard at work on the treadmill beside his desk when his chief political advisor Raymond Kove walked in briskly, unannounced.

"Mr. President, I have an idea that will make everyone completely re-evaluate your entire administration, a new achievement, something that will transcend the election, and even Iraq."

"Transcend Iraq? I know you think readin' all those books makes you smart, but you're starting to sound like you been breathin' too much of that Ivory Tower air. Transcend Iraq? How, R.K.?"

"Mr. President, your legacy could be in a tad of trouble unless we do something new and creative, and do it soon."

"Okay, R.K., out with it!"

"As I say, it's something that will really impress people, something the world would never expect from you, something that will rally our core, woo the west, and, unbelievably enough, it will also win over the Muslims. Sir, you'll be able to walk off tall and proud, having won your legacy through this vehicle. It'll be like insurance."

"You've got somethin' that can do all that?"

"Yes, sir."

"You're not goin' to make me admit any more mistakes."

"Perish the thought."

"Or change a hair of policy."

"Absolutely not."

"So what is it, R.K.? If you don't get to the point you're really going to get me riled, and you don't want to be here for that."

"Mr. President," and again Raymond Kove looked off in the distance, as if he really could see the future clear and shapely as the cumulus cloud hanging above Lafayette Park. "Mr. President, I think you should write a book. It can be one of such power it will rally the Muslims in Iraq, remind the Europeans they have to love us no matter what we do, stop the Hispanics from messing with the border, unite America, make us hearken back to our previous glories, and inspire us to new ones. You will secure your legacy through ...fiction! Literature! You'll write a western! A western novel.

"Imagine, Mr. President, a great Christian cowboy—I don't think any-one's written anything like this before—and he's a great fighter and leader and even healer, and maybe he's been to the holy land on his adventures before he appears in our book. Sir, I guarantee it will get you a whole new image."

"You done lot of guaranteein' during the last seven years, Raymond, and we've been eatin' a lot of crow for it."

"This is different, sir. My people have done their homework, and they tell me no president has ever written a novel while still in office. And the best part is that you can achieve great things, like bring the Jews and the Muslims together for a peace plan in the Palestine of the book, even if you can't do it over there in the real Middle East."

"A peace plan?"

"Yes, sir. This project will give you a chance to get it out there, and with no bad consequences whatsoever because it will all be between the pages of a novel. All kinds of issues. Heck, you might even get nominated for the No-bel Peace Prize. And if the book's as good as I think we can make it, the lit-erature prize at the same time."

The President jogged on as he cogitated his aide's words. "You don't really mean for me to put the words down myself, do you, pardner?"

"No, sir. I don't."

"Then how we gonna do this, Raymond?"

"We will find you the perfect ghostwriter."

Two

A.B. Konig was riding his rusty green bicycle up a slight incline into a drenching, wind-driven rain. He lifted off his seat, wobbled, leaned, tipped, then halted and re-mounted, pedaling on just as a particularly nasty gust smacked him head-on. The brim of his ancient Washington Senators base-ball cap stuck out from underneath his helmet and dripped heavily onto the tip of his long nose. Konig tilted up his eyes and took in, through oval lenses, the roof of the White House in the distance. It seemed to shimmer in the wet afternoon light but then disappeared beneath a half dozen wispy plumes of dark, threatening cloud.

A lime-colored VW, like a well-hit tennis ball, sped by in a blur within two inches of killing him. Konig shook himself into alertness, and pedaled on. "You're a ghost-rider as well as a ghostwriter," he mumbled aloud. Liking his invention, he repeated it, and then added truth to wordplay: "You're almost invisible, aren't you?"

He often conducted such meetings and imagined conversations with himself as he rode. Other regularly appearing guests were his ancient aunt Emma and his wife Anna, and these voices were beginning to assemble around him now like a fantasy Team Konig, cheering and spouting advice, both requested and not, as they cycled alongside or behind him on the busy D.C. streets.

"We're in some rut, Benjamin." This was his wife Anna, the sweetest of all of the voices in Konig's psychological chorus. "A big wide one." It was as if Anna were within inches of him on her old Peugeot racer. "Aren't you worried that a rut can widen into a path, a road, a whole life, a marriage? Our conundrum, our connubial partnership." Anna was a poet. She kept tossing out the words, like arrows toward a target, until the right one stuck. "A so-called union. A misfire. A mess. A—"

"—Enough," Konig said to her, although she was not really there to hear his riposte. "How could it be a rut if I love you?"

"Oh, Benjamin, I think that your love is altering even when it alteration finds."

He had fallen in love with Anna a dozen years ago—he was fortyish then, and she ten years younger, but both had foolish first marriages behind them—when she was working as a waitress. He now could see out the small clear corner of his foggy glasses the very restaurant, the Failed Vegetarian, with its stuccoed bunch of celery and carrots above the door where they had met. Nearly ten years of marriage later, and despite a graduate degree in poetry writing, which the income from Konig's oddball books had made possible for Anna to complete, she still waited tables a few days a week to supplement the increasingly meager proceeds of his ghostwriting career. With only a small chapbook and a few obscure periodical publications, however, Anna was growing just a bit frustrated; she was certain she had a big book percolating if only she could get a break. Anna usually made the best of it by writing down fragments of conversations she jotted down on the backs of customers' checks, which she later incorporated into her poetry.

To the best of his understanding, what Anna did was use words like notes of music or dabs of paint on the page, or maybe her language might also be likened to these cold drops of rain that kept coming at Konig as he rode, running down his collar now, sliding down his nose, some drops wetter than others, some heavier, some light and quick or ticklish, others leaving their slow saturated trail down his back:

> Falling Frisbee a cold canal
> Where bees once lived. Yeats. Forget
> His loudness. A death-soft glade. Interior. Shift.
> Green the council overrules the air
> Slow the worm parts your hair
> Nothing brother or sister Free Dame
> Nothing is there

He had once committed to memory large chunks of what Anna wrote, and had recited sections to her during their courtship and when they made love. Yes, I am aware it has been, alas, quite a while since the last recital. See you tonight, Anna.

The rain grew heavier as he rode on, and now Konig was surprised to hear from his Auntie Emma. Here she was, at nearly a hundred years old, the oldest female anti-war activist in Washington D.C., and perhaps the whole world, pulling up alongside him, opposite Anna, on an old bike she often borrowed from President William McKinley's wife Ida. Auntie Emma had a habit of plausible exaggeration, asserting also, for example, that she had helped Emma Lazarus out with her verse when she was a little girl. Born in 1908, Emma's math simply didn't add up for her to have been a bicycle pal of Ida McKinley or the helper to the other Emma, but Auntie Emma never much bothered with the details. That, along with her age, very frail skeletal structure, foul mouth, and very volatile anarchist temperament made Konig think twice before crossing or correcting his great-aunt, even in conversations he invented while riding in the pouring rain.

"You are acting like an ass, an idiot," Emma went after him with her all-too-frequent rebukes. "You are going to lose that girl. Mark my word. You'll see. Since marriage is almost always a losing proposition for women, to hell with that institution! It's just as well that Anna divorces you. Maybe I'll help her, you corporate lackey."

As she cursed him, Konig began to brake. He believed a bicycle should observe all the rules of the road applicable to four-wheeled vehicles, and he now came to a sliding stop beneath the red light swaying on its cable above him. He let imaginary Auntie Emma pedal on into the busy intersection, where she disappeared into the drizzle and silence. This riding in the bad weather, he cogitated as he waited, somehow suited him. True, he was relatively slow and rode without much panache, a bit like a messenger who has lost his way. Yet he was also neither fearful nor short on doggedness, and was this not also somehow a reflection of his life and oddball career? Konig took off his cap, loosened his ponytail, which seemed to have gathered more water than a mop, shook it out, and then breathed deeply.

The light changed and Konig pedaled on across the street and across the stream of his recollections. True, viewed objectively, Emma's warning was apt, if hurtful, because Anna was absolutely right to consider that he may not have turned out to be the greatest husband. To his considerable surprise, he had begun to forget significant dates in their lives, did not always listen with much sympathy to Anna's tales of woe from the restaurant—was devolving into, at best, a B-minus of a husband. Complicating this, his ghostwriter's earnings had lately gone into a serious tailspin. He didn't need them to keep hectoring him to know the facts. Still in all, Anna and Emma were his family, and Konig almost always looked forward to coming home to them, especially to his wife, who occasionally still recited her new poems to him:

> Clog. Athwart. Believe me.
> Lowlife bays. Moon retreats.
> By day the waters lap the billboard.

Was he fooling himself that they still inhabited together a kind of wordy bower, where, after the old lady went to sleep, the sex was still pretty good too? Absolutely. Be truthful now, Konig. Well, at least maybe, okay, some of the time. What was undeniable was that as the door to Writing Trouble seemed to be opening even wider, Love Trouble was getting a leg up and in danger of rushing right in.

For Konig had fallen, professionally, on embarrassingly bad times of late, the extent of which he tried to conceal from his family. After he'd left his long-time job at a public relations agency and had gone out on his own, anticipated clients had not come over to him.

Deciding that public relations was not all that different from simply making things up, Konig switched to fiction, and made a promising start. He became the writer of several off-the-beaten-track but gritty westerns. They were usually about heroes who found ways of overcoming unusual, even impossible obstacles. Although sales were middling to mediocre, there had been one exciting prospect, a movie option for a two hundred pager called *Vengeance Valley Days*. Konig considered that story—the tale of a partially blind, handicapped gunfighter regaining his prowess through murder and mayhem—far from his best. After two on-again-off-again years of development, the film was never made.

However, there was eventually so little money to be made in the genre fiction racket and it took such labor to create what he considered even a mediocre potboiler that Konig, reassessing yet again, shifted career streams, and threw himself into the more lucrative—so he thought—and more respectable jack-of-all-trades writer-for-hire business of ghostwriting.

He penned a book on bird-watching for bright eleven-year-olds; he devised a fundraising brochure to help fight a disease; he novelized a movie about a vampire ferret; and, finally, he accepted a job arranged by his agent (now long-gone and fled to Bolivia, having embezzled three thousand dollars of precious royalties from Konig) for a project, *When Candy Was King*, which told the family saga of a man who insisted a distant entrepreneurial cousin had invented the lollipop in 1857 at a candy shop high on a hill in New Haven.

The irony was that this book had been Konig's best-selling effort thus far. After three or four more forgettable volumes, even by his own diminished standards, and even for a ghostwriter working, admittedly, on the bottom rung of the low end of the vanity market, he was not doing very well. Now and then Konig even borrowed lunch money from Anna's tips and, even more embarrassingly, from Emma's pension.

Feeling irritable, very wet, and now filled with a low-grade guilt (or was it just a fever coming on, occasioned by these recollections?), Konig waved goodbye and sent Team Konig riding swiftly home. Taking advantage of a lull in the wind, he pedaled the remaining blocks to his office in excellent time.

Konig shouldered his bicycle and began to descend the steps to his space, 120 square feet between the boiler room and bathroom in the base-ment of the law firm of Cheever, Einstein, and Bell. There was no longer any Einstein, but Bell and Cheever, two Washington insiders with ties to the Oval Office, kept Einstein on the marquee, they said, because it sug-gested they were geniuses.

Cheever and Bell had wanted to charge Konig $300 rent for the space because the lawyers would have had to clear out and store elsewhere their boxes of old records. However, in one of the most successful negotiations of his business life, Konig had bargained them down to $150, suggesting he didn't mind the boxes at all, which, once they agreed, he moved to the far corner of the basement, where, stacked and untouched, they now teetered like a little legal ziggurat.

Konig bought a seven-foot-high rice paper and wood-slatted Japanese screen and placed it decorously between the lawyers' boxes and his own tiny yet efficient work area—desk and table with computer, lamp, and printer, kilim rug, several chairs, small bookcase, and numerous milk crates full of stuff. There was also an old red futon left over from some previous inhabi-tant, which Cheever let him have for nothing, and which was suitable for napping; it was well used. In this manner, Konig had ended up, happily, with precisely what he really needed, a comfortable, utilitarian space including phone and computer lines, all for still under $200 per month.

"When your ship comes in, Konig," Cheever had told him, "you can rent the entire basement."

Konig didn't mind being in the basement with lawyers above him. He especially enjoyed the busy footsteps of Sandra and Sharon, the paralegal twins who, from his underground audio vantage, seemed even to walk in sync, tapping reassuringly on the ceiling above. The basement was usually warm in winter, cool in summer, and then there was Norman.

Konig propped his bicycle against the wall, opened his office door, hung his wet outerwear on the coat rack by the threshold, then found the switch and flicked on the light. He whispered, "Good morning, Norman," and paused to hear an answer.

The mouse remained silent, and Konig stepped over two milk crates and around other boxes crammed with folders, an athletic bag with an extra helmet and riding gear, and approached his desk. Here were yet more piles of paper, but at least the area around the computer was clear. Along one side of the computer were three yellow and red coffee cans, each sprouting a dozen or so pencils, their sharp points angled up and out, both a convenience and an inadvertent danger and warning for the writer's overreaching hand. Occasionally Norman lurked here. Konig withdrew from his bag several folders, placed them on the desk beside the computer, and sat.

Nearby were a second small table with phone and Rolodex, and more files. Two blue folding director's chairs were beyond, and, beside them, the red futon that today could not even be sat upon for the line-up of storage boxes that filled and sagged it end to end.

Settling himself in his chair, Konig inclined forward. "Good morning, Norman," he repeated, but this time he was rewarded with an answering rustle among the papers and books. Although the ghostwriter did not see the small gray creature he considered his pet and assistant, Konig knew he was nearby.

Working here, underground, on material of not much pitch or moment, Konig somehow found a way to remain an optimist. He spent perhaps more time than he should searching for the mouse and, in the process, weighing the good and the bad in his life. Yet he usually arrived, without the aid of external intoxicants, at a mild-mannered acceptance of himself: he was no longer going to change the world through his former, mostly college-based and great-way-to-meet-wild-girls-based radicalism, or through his challenging prose. Instead, he was simply a writer, at his best light and amusing, who was really quite adept at the superficial, and, moreover, believed firmly that the superficial too deserved its rightful place in the world. Konig, of course, still nurtured the hope that his ship would come in, provided, of course, a ship could somehow find its way to a basement. If the tsunami in Asia and

Katrina in New Orleans were any measure, this was more and more of a possibility.

The only live projects Konig had going for him now, however, were ghosting the rags-to-riches memoir of the first Jew to break into a blue-blood Washington-area country club; and the second project, a history of crowns, that is, of the dental variety, which Konig's oral surgeon was allegedly writing.

Although it troubled Konig that he had not yet independently been able to corroborate the Jewish social pioneer's claim and that project was therefore a bit stalled, still the saga was paying cash. As to the dentist, Konig had foolishly accepted payment in kind, which meant that, in addition to very poor cash flow, he frequently also had a sore mouth.

Still, Konig bucked himself up, often by vicariously addressing the mouse with daily morning pep talks intended for himself: Soon we will sell something. Right, Norman? Soon, we will both have new clients. Some brie for you and some new big cheese for me to write about. Then, when Anna calls, we'll say, confidently, Darling, did *Poetry* get back to you yet? No, then, screw them. Why not go all the way and try *The New Yorker*? Did you get any acceptances this afternoon?

And if she hasn't, I will tell her, Honey, don't get down on yourself, and don't despair, because both of us here appreciate you and the work. And things are looking up today. Very soon some income will be percolating here. Yes, Norman and I have both had some good soundings. And...Konig heard a rustle of paper underfoot and then saw a flash of gray behind the computer console.

"Norman, what do you think?"

In the inevitable silence that followed these inquiries, Konig concluded the mouse had his own assignments, maybe even a deadline. Taking the small but useful inspiration from his mouse, the ghostwriter sighed, and got down to work.

Three

"Who are my very favorite authors?" President George was asking his wife Lenore, on the following day, as he climbed the presidential Stairmaster with the determination of a Sir Edmund Hillary mounting the last icy face of an Everest. "You know how I am with names."

The First Lady, dressed in gray sweatpants and a flattering deep red sweatshirt, was pumping five-pound hand weights.

He had told her about the western novel project shortly after the meeting with Raymond Kove, and Lenore said she thought it was a splendid idea. He always got encouraged when Lenore liked one of his ideas, and when she said 'splendid,' that was a real endorsement. Big Time.

"Well," she said, placing her hand weights down on the carpet, "you used to like the western novels of this fellow, Konig. A.B. Konig. You remember? He wrote a novel called *Vengeance Valley Days*, and I recollect you reading that with unusual concentration and relish."

"Maybe I'll give this Konig a tryout."

"I think that's a very wise choice," Lenore said, as she resumed lifting.

Four

When Konig arrived home that evening, he looked down from the bottom of his stoop, as he often did, hoping to see a light on in the mullioned window of the basement apartment. It would indicate Paramahansa Yogan might indeed be home. Yogan was a diminutive reclusive brown man, a low-level diplomat from the small Muslim island nation of Brawada, newly admitted to the U.N., to whom they had rented the space a year ago.

When Konig heard a strain of sitar-ish music rising from below, he decided to make an effort to redeem the day, which had turned out badly. He knocked on the door to see if he could collect Paramahansa's overdue rent.

As he rapped a second time, the music shut off. "Mr. Ambassador," Konig raised his voice to be heard through the door, "it's Konig, the landlord."

Paramahansa was obviously making him wait, and why not? So was everyone else in his life, it seemed. Earlier, he had indeed experienced one of the most intensely non-revenue-producing seven hours of his life. The oral surgeon had decided to terminate his contract, and he was so peeved he had sent, along with his letter of cancellation, in a lumpy envelope, a still damp impression of Konig's rotting molar. Konig had already put in two months of research, without pay. To get any cash, he would have the very disagreeable task of suing the dentist. Yet wasn't his time worth more than a hunk of wet clay?

Now, tonight, before he ascended to see Anna, was it too much to imagine that the Ambassador, as they called him, might give him some cash in hand, or a check?

"Please open. I won't bite."

Konig, who loved basements (the inhabiting of which must, he guessed, have run deep in the family's genes), had reluctantly given up this space, which he and Anna had previously used for their library. It was a decision forced on them when their income began to decline the last two cold winters. Emma let them live in the house rent-free, but her pension was modest, and she expected to be reasonably warm; and the proceeds of language poetry and ghostwriting were, not unremarkably, insufficient to keep up with the rising heating bills.

They had placed an ad in the paper, and Paramahansa had replied. He said he was a diplomat from a very small country, an atoll really. Indeed, in the beginning, he was so diplomatically reticent about his country, Brawada, and about himself, they thought he might have something to hide. As if reading their minds, he told them how many times he had already been turned down, how difficult it was these days for a dark Muslim man, even an ambassador, to find proper lodging in the nation's capital.

It came as a disconcerting surprise to the Konig family that Brawada was so colossally poor, that paying their small percentage of U.N. dues usually meant that there was little or no money left to pay Yogan's rent to Emma and to Konig. Still, Konig and Anna liked the man and his warm smile, and so did Emma.

To make ends meet, Paramahansa gave meditation and yoga lessons in the basement, which Anna and Emma often took as barter. Was he a diplomat from a country so poor and small that he supplemented with the yoga, or was Paramahansa rather a full-time yoga instructor moonlighting as a diplomat? Konig could not figure out which. Regardless, the rent was always late, and getting later.

Finally Konig heard the scrape of a chair. "I know you're in there, Mr. Ambassador. Any chance for a few bucks this month?"

"I don't think so, good sir. Maybe next."

"Maybe next?"

"Yes, if the gods are with us and bring our island good crops and peace. Your beautiful wife and Auntie had major success this morning modulating their breathing while doing the spider."

"I'm so glad to hear that," Konig said. "How about twenty-five?"

"Too steep."

"Twenty?"

"How profoundly I, on behalf of my countrymen and countrywomen, would like to pay in full, but we are unable to do so at the present time. Perhaps in the near future, when our elders return to the council."

"Fifteen?"

"Brawada may be able to contribute something in a smaller range. Would five be permissible?"

"The entire exchequer of your country cannot afford fifteen bucks, sir?"

"Ten?"

"Ten it is."

The door opened now, and the Ambassador emerged, a man who reminded Konig of Sam Jaffe when he played the ageless mystic in *Shangri-La*. "Here you are, good sir. And profound thanks for your indulgence, Mr. Konig."

Konig unwrinkled the bill and nodded, as Paramahansa retreated back into his basement. "We must attend to some dispatches."

"Of course we must."

"Until we meet again. And please give your lovely wife and much revered Aunt Emma our affectionate wishes."

"Oh, I will for sure."

As Konig climbed the steps, he heard the door open below. "And a receipt would be most appreciated, Mr. A.B. Konig. At your profound convenience."

Five

From the foyer, where he began rapidly to change, Konig could see his aunt and Anna sitting beneath the green-shaded lamp suspended over a small card table in the middle of the room and playing Scrabble. Even seated, they were like a cactus and a rose, Emma still close to six feet tall, in a pair of slippers and a flimsy dress, and almost always prickly. Anna, in a red bathrobe, made word sounds out loud: "Rat, rhumba, bum, humbug."

"Don't tip me off, dear."

"Oh you beat me all the time, Emma. What difference does it make? You're so smart."

"Harm, hub…rub."

After changing quickly into jeans and a sweatshirt, Konig approached the players. He often saw little difference between the words arrayed on the Scrabble board and Anna's poetry, but that observation, made only once, was never welcome again. "Should I play?"

"Shut up, please."

"Emma, he's a nice boy," Anna said.

"Says who!"

"Says me and I'm married to him."

"Really?"

"You do acknowledge that we're married, Auntie."

"Yes, yes, and a sorry goddam development that is."

Anna smiled wanly and indulgently at Konig, and the sweetness of her face always—well, almost always—softened the sting of Emma's tongue. Anna was diminutive, hardly more than 115 pounds, but very strong, with powerful shoulders and muscles from her workouts. She often carried Emma up and down the flight of well-worn wooden steps that led to the old lady's suite of rooms.

"Home is the ghostwriter," Konig said expansively, "home from the sea. And was it ever pouring!" He peered over the board. "I did manage to get some rent money from Paramahansa. Ten bucks."

"That much?" Anna said, paying more attention to the board.

"Why don't you leave that poor man alone?"

"He's our tenant, Emma. Your tenant."

"Out of my light," Emma snapped back at him. "Ten will not make or break us, will it? Now move your leprous, foul presence."

Konig took a deep, long breath of self-restraint. "Good words, ladies," he said as he circled around the table. "Let me see. 'Arse,' 'bastard,' and, what's this 'shithead'? I assume these are your contributions, Emma. Say, is 'shithead' really a word?"

"It's a compound noun made up of 'shit' and 'head.' You trying to confuse me, A.B.? You always forget you're dealing with the head of the Dewitt Clinton High School English Department, and back in '98. 1898, we didn't suffer foolish students gladly."

"Come on, Aunt Emma. You weren't even born 1898."

"Don't tell me when I was born, shithead. Of course it's a word. It also happens to be you! Now move out of my light, you dope fiend."

"Calm down. I am many things but a drug addict is not among them."

"Parasite."

"How your great-aunt loves you, A.B.," Anna said. "Her curses are her kisses. How's Norman?"

Konig pulled the chair in snugly between the two women in his life. "Norman is doing great. He sends you his love, Auntie."

"You two should have children instead of sitting around every night discussing a rat."

Konig summoned the patience to tell his great-aunt for the several millionth time. "M-o-u-s-e."

"Mouse, rat, they're all quick little fuckers scamper under your dress."

"For godsake," said Konig.

"For godsake, for godsake," Emma mimicked. Then she said, "Just look at that." She leaned over and rearranged her letters. "S-o-n-u-v-a-b-i-t-c-h. Twenty points. Sonuvabitch."

"What Anna would like to know," Anna said, "is how you two did not end up killing each other before I entered the picture."

"She was affectionate to me before we got married. She's transferred all that to you, and now I'm a birdbrain, numbskull, idiot, and dope fiend."

"And sonuvabitch. Have I told you about how Emma Lazarus stole lines from me in that poetry competition? That girl could use only ten-dollar words. I had to teach her how to love the common man and write for him. What's up there on the Statue of Liberty is really my stuff. Have I told you what she did is complete plagiarism?"

"Yes you have, Emma. Several hundred times."

"Well goddam I'm going to tell you again. I'm going to petition that birdbrain president to give me credit. I haven't lived a hundred years for nothing."

"I think he might be a little too busy to get back to you," Anna said.

"You two play on," Konig said. "I'm going to prepare dinner."

"What's it going to be?" Emma snapped. "The usual?"

"Macaroni and cheese."

"You two should be feeding me better for all the money I slip you."

"It's the people's food," said Konig. "Anyway, you don't need teeth to eat it."

At the doorway to the kitchen, where Anna and Konig now set to work preparing a salad, they sat Emma down on a stool with *The Nation*, to which she was a lifelong subscriber. She liked being on the edge of the action in the kitchen, and from the threshold she commented on the news. Invariably the object of her attack was President Brewster George. "Never in my life-time, children, and I go way back to when that little gnome from Ohio, William McKinley, and T.R. launched the Spanish-American War...Why, Clara Barton and Emma and I picketed on Pennsylvania Avenue..."

"You weren't born yet, Emma."

"Never, never have we had such a...such a...numbskull. Why, everyone knows the Spanish no more planted a bomb on the *Maine* than Saddam Hussein had WMD. This president is the worst ever. Do you hear me?"

"We do, Emma. And so do the neighbors."

"Well, good. Everyone should hear that this president is worse even than James Polk and Millard Fillmore, and I knew James and Millard well. How's that macaroni and cheese coming?"

"Going to be yummy," said Anna. "When you're done, you'll have a bath and then bed."

"No goddam bath for me. That's for sissies."

"Oh yes?" Konig said.

"I'm not taking a bath until we kick that man out of the White House... What do you say to that?"

"Look who takes his place. You're cutting off your nose to spite your face."

"I never understood that idiomatic usage," Anna said.

"There's a lot you children don't understand. Here's what I never got: How you allow that sonuvabitch to steal an election, start a war, walk on the Constitution, and he gets away with it? What's wrong with your generation? I say, Impeach, Impeach."

"Enough politics. Let's have dinner, Emma," Konig said, helping her into the bright light of the kitchen. "Speaking of which, at the end of the day, as I was leaving, Sharon and Sandra told me, of all things, that Cheever wants to speak with me tomorrow morning."

"About what?" said Anna.

"I have no idea. Never happened before that I've had a formal appointment."

"Maybe he doesn't like you keeping that rat in his basement. Even the capitalists have a right to live without vermin. Goddam."

"Auntie, can I ask you, please," Konig said, as he sipped the red wine he had poured in three large glasses, "just one little question?"

"Is it about that brazen hussy Emma Lazarus and how she stole lines from me, my goddam lines—Give me your tired, your poor, your masses yearning to breathe free—my goddam lines she stole and submitted in her sonnet, and it won, and did she give me credit? No."

"It's not about the other Emma, Emma. It's about you."

"Oh."

"Yes, why must you swear so much?"

"Because I goddam like the sound of it."

"Enough!" Konig shouted.

"It's good for her to let it rip," Anna said. "All that vitriol, it keeps your Auntie fit."

"Hells bells, I'm fit as you are, and I'm at least hundred years your senior, little girl. Don't get me started."

"You're not even started yet?" asked Konig. "Where's my helmet?"

When dinner was over, Anna cradled Emma in her arms and carried her upstairs, where she finally submitted to a bath, and fell quickly asleep. When Konig emerged from his shower and slipped into bed and put his arm out to grab the pointed crop of Anna's hair and tug on it gently to see if she was interested, she was already sleeping, and had even begun to snore.

As the ghostwriter inserted his small white beeswax earplugs and drifted off, he wondered how such a small woman could produce such a locomotive-caliber noise; and also what in the world was the meaning of life on the planet, of his life in particular; and, specifically, what Mr. Cheever might have to say to him tomorrow.

Six

Cheever, a man of average height who appeared taller for his slimness and the tailored suits he wore, had blazingly white hair cut short and always just slightly tousled, that sat on his head like a patch of snow. Bell was his physical opposite, a short man shaped not quite eponymously but rotund, with steeply sloping shoulders, a perpetually sweaty brow, as nervous and chatty as Cheever was confident and severe.

They had in common, however, that they each were one of twins and they were so enamored of the condition—found life with a double to be an excellent background and natural source of training in their previous secret work in the State Department and Foreign Service—that they often hired twins as their paralegals. Sharon and Sandra, who now stood at the top of Konig's basement steps, were the third or fourth pair who had worked at Cheever, Einstein, and Bell since Konig had begun renting.

"Would you like coffee?" one of the twins called down to him.

"Yes, please," Konig said as he tried to locate Norman among his piles.

The twins might have phoned in their question, but for economy's sake and since so few people were calling him, Konig had disconnected his local service two months before.

"Milk, Mr. K?"

"Yes."

"Whole? Two percent, one percent, or skim?"

Had he not been distracted, Konig would have been bewildered by all this unaccustomed solicitude. "Oh," he mumbled to himself as he searched for Norman among the boxes of dental crown research, now pushed into the far corner. "Anything." Then, suddenly, Konig lost his balance, lunged, and tripped over the straps of a backpack stuffed with old manuscripts and a broken bicycle pump.

"You okay down there, Mr. K?"

"Everything under control here. Make it skim."

Konig had only wanted to feed Norman—and maybe stroke his back for good luck. He had only a few minutes before leaving for the mystery meeting at a still undisclosed location, which Cheever had told him was occurring this morning. Now here he was, oddly, delaying, and here he also now lay on the floor in his only good suit, which Anna had made him wear today, a brown three-piece with stripes, a little too gaudy and with the vest missing, something of a Carnaby Street holdover from the 1960s that he had purchased on a trip to London some years ago. Now he was fairly well covered with fuzz from his insufficiently vacuumed carpet.

"Whenever you're ready," one of the twins yelled down to him.

He hurriedly brushed himself off. "Up in a moment."

Upstairs, Cheever checked his wristwatch and Bell his pocket watch. They were standing halfway down the stoop of the building, looking up. Below them, idling at the curb, a limousine, long as a schooner, with blue-tinted windows, waited.

"Can you believe it?" said Cheever *sotto voce.*

"The President," whispered Bell.

"But Kove didn't want to chat with me. Not at all. Very unusual 'Just bring A.B. Konig,' he said."

"You asked him why?"

"Of course. Indeed, I asked him why, although I didn't use that term, that word, *why*, but my implication was clearly: why? I mean what the hell for? The man doesn't even have a telephone. Doesn't own a proper suit. Did you see what he's got on? Is there a carnival in town? What could they possibly want with him?"

"Exactly. What does the President of the United States want with a man who is so...out of touch...whatever he does down there. Say, what does he do down there?"

"Evasive as all get out."

"Who? Konig?"

"No. Kove."

"Unbelievable."

"And we're not to talk about it, Kove said."

"Directly or indirectly. We're to keep it under our hats."

"That'll be easy because we don't know a thing."

"Nothing, except we're going to be late. Where in the world is that fool?"

"We're messenger boys."

"Yes. On the other hand, let's look on the positive side. He's a man from our basement, right? And we're doing a service in having provided the basement for the man who is headed for the White House to perform some kind of service, which we don't know anything about, although we should. That's a service too in a way. Konig has done some work for us, hasn't he? Now and then."

"Now and then he proofreads with the girls. He jokes. They giggle a lot when he shows up."

"Well, that's it. We've trained him, then. Given him some skills. Some of the wherewithal that he is going to employ on whatever it is Kove wants him to do."

"I get your point. I still say we're messenger boys. What in the world is taking him so long?"

"You better call Kove. I'll go down to haul him out of there."

Just as Cheever turned to fetch him, Konig emerged from the building into the long diagonals of light that fell on the stoop. As his eye took in the limousine and Cheever and Bell, who turned to face him, they appeared to Konig like a couple of sentries who were just about to take up their positions.

"Mr. Konig, please. We have an appointment."

"I've been waiting for you to tell me where."

"You'll see. Just step in the car."

"What's the problem, Mr. Konig?"

"You tell me. Have I done something wrong?"

"On the contrary. Apparently you've done something very right, although what that is...well, I'm sure you will illuminate us."

"You want me in that boat?"

"Please. Yes. The limo. We'll talk about it inside."

"On the way."

"Have you ever seen *Three Days of the Condor?* Robert Redford, Faye Dunaway, and Max von Sydow? The agency. The company. You guys know stuff like that. It was on TV last night. I couldn't sleep. This is weird. I don't feel comfortable stepping into that limo unless you tell me exactly where we're going."

"What's come over you, Mr. Konig?"

Konig wasn't quite sure either. It might have been the residual paranoia from having watched the movie late into the night, or that he had not eaten much for breakfast, or the fall he took lunging for Norman. For he felt woozy and sensed that these men, Cheever and Bell, with whom he rarely exchanged a word, were not to be trusted. Suddenly he imagined them in trench coats. The butts of their guns made visible bulges, and didn't they also have those listening devices in their ears?

Konig went up to Cheever and wound his gaze around the suspect ear. It was exceedingly well scrubbed, almost to a roseate shine, but empty of wires. He did the same to Bell's ear. "Can you please tell me where I'm being ferried?"

"You're hardly cargo, Mr. Konig," said Bell.

As the two men moved closer to him. Cheever whispered, "You have been summoned to the White House."

"White House? What's the joke?"

"Exactly. We thought you might tell us."

"I can't imagine what they want from me."

"Come, come, Konig."

"There must be some really big misunderstanding," Konig maneuvered himself away from the limo. "Am I being audited?"

"The President of the United States does not personally conduct audits."

"At least, to the best of our knowledge, and not at the White House."

"Something is wrong with this picture. I need to get out."

"Calm down, Mr. Konig."

When they slid into the limousine and he inhaled its warm, luxurious, leathery smell, the dissident genes of Konig's great-aunt and those of his own union organizer parents (alas, both deceased) seemed suddenly to well up. All the DNA of those in Emma's line who had mistrusted and feared the government activated themselves in Konig. Having lain dormant for decades since his oddball activism in college, these forces now instantly incubated in the limo, reared up in his system, and demanded their due. "I'm sorry," he declared. "I'm not cooperating with this. Let the President spend his time on Iraq and begging the world's forgiveness. He doesn't need to meet with me. Please."

"Stop fidgeting with the windows, Mr. Konig, and calm yourself," said Bell.

"Something's wrong. I want out. I prefer not to go."

"You what?"

"I prefer not to go."

"You *prefer* not to go?"

"Well, there's something fishy going on here. You just don't show up at the White House. Why didn't I get an invitation, an explanation, a chance to defend myself. Or at least a call?"

"If you had a phone down there, maybe the President could have left you a message."

"Well, tell him I'm happy to hear from him from time to time, but the car, the secrecy, it's making me, well, you see, a little jumpy. You guys can understand that, can't you? What does the President want from me?"

"Why are you laughing?"

"Completely inappropriate. Sorry. I always laugh like this when I think I'm losing my mind."

"Now, Mr. Konig, let's alleviate your concern. The way we see it, your president calls, you answer. The reason, the subject, they'll make it clear in time. I'll tell you for certain this is no audit. That much we know. And that's all we know. You're going to the residence. The private entrance. "

"Oh no I'm not," said Konig. "I'm taking a walk."

He climbed with alacrity over Bell's knees, opened the door, and scampered onto the curb. Without looking back, he accelerated down the sidewalk. He would have broken into a run if he hadn't felt completely foolish and certain he would have tripped over the floppy cuffs of his suit. He headed quickly home.

Shaking their heads in disbelief, Cheever and Bell re-entered their offices and directed Sharon to call Raymond Kove at the White House. When the presidential advisor called back moments later, a long conversation ensued, in which Cheever talked—he mainly listened and made affirmative noises—

while Bell stood by with his thumbs in the pockets of his vest leaning toward his partner. As the positive nods and "yes, sirs" mounted, he urged him on, for a telephonic negotiation had begun.

When Cheever hung up, a robust glow of satisfaction seemed to light him up in a full-body halo. His face, beneath the tufts of white hair and thick eyebrows, appeared positively rosy.

"Kove told me the whole thing. They have a project for Konig. Some sort of writing assignment. Top secret stuff. Loony, if you ask me, but you can't argue with Kove. On the other hand, why the President keeps listening to him…I mean if Kove said, Let's invade Canada, George would say, When? Go figure. Anyway, they want our tenant to write a book. Presidential legacy or some such. And what's more, when I told Kove how skittish Konig seemed, how he wanted it all laid out in advance, and how he seemed really nervous about even showing up, not flattered at all and how, without some…cultivation they might not get their man at all, well, guess what?"

"We are being retained?"

"Yes, indeed, my friend. We are in harness again. For some reason they think that ridiculous fellow is critical to the President's final days in office. We are to explain it carefully, calmly, and bring him in from the cold for the President to make the final sale."

"Shouldn't be so hard."

"Piece of cake."

"And the fee?"

"Ample. Generous."

"We're no longer messenger boys, are we?"

Seven

"So how's it goin'?" the President asked Raymond Kove, "with our scribe, our man Konig?"

"Well, no matter how we cut it, I believe Konig's going to be a hard nut to crack."

"I am gettin' just a tad impatient with not gettin' what I want. I think Konig and I will get along great. This could be a new classic. Say, what should we call the book, R.K.? How's about…*Ridin' to Riyadh?*"

"Catchy, Mr. President."

"Now what other temporary obstacles did your boys uncover that we will simply have to overcome with A.B. Konig?"

"Well, his great-aunt, she's certified CPR, sir"

"CPR? Hell, that's not an obstacle. That's good. Why is havin' a great-aunt who knows cardiopulmonary resuscitation a problem, R.K.? Did you loose up a screw the other day when we went runnin'?"

"CPR. As in Communist Party of America, Revolutionary division. Dropped out in 1939, but still…"

"…CPR. I get it. Uh-oh."

Silence enveloped them, and then, very slowly, a noise found its way in through one of the few open windows at the White House. "B.G.! B.G.! Biggest Killer in American History!" Kove tucked his clipboard under an arm, and closed the window. The President did twenty-five jumping jacks, and felt better. Kove studied his notes.

"Okay, give me more," the President panted. "There must be a missus. Doesn't somebody in the family want to make some money? There must be a way in."

"Konig's wife is a poet. Painter and nurse practitioner in the past and now waitress and poet. There appears to be a certain amount of pecuniary difficulty. Yes."

"Right. So, to summarize, sir: We have the ghostwriter, we have the wife who is a poet, we have some kind of old lady Raging-Grannies-Cindy Sheehan-type great-auntie, oh, and we have a little Muslim diplomat all under the same roof. That's it, sir."

"Well, we can work with these people. I feel for them. Especially for the ghostwriter. I feel a lot of compassion boiling up inside. I know A.B.'s not rackin' up the contracts, right?"

"Oh, absolutely not, Mr. President. Let me see, the IRS documents here indicate over the last three years, he's averaged $3,400 a year revenue from the writing. His wife's waitressing income is largely unreported. I guess we could work that angle, prosecute for tax evasion if you like. She also last year earned 153 dollars. Sonnets, haikus, pantoums. That sort of thing."

"Pan who?"

"Pantoums. Poetry, sir. The $153 was publishing income from two poems published in *Oink* and *Expletive*. Those are two magazines, one online."

"All right, Raymond. Here's how I figger: We make the poetess happy with a real publication, no more of this oinking, and then we offer Konig some big bucks too. I mean serious money. We also threaten to deport the old lady back to Hungary or wherever old commies are huddlin' these days, and we check out this Muslim in the basement and see what we got on him; and then we have a plan, don't we?"

"A plan, sir."

"Then implement it. Aren't I providin' the leadership? Do I have to do everything?"

Eight

After the incident with the limousine, Konig found himself unable to go into his office. He was now on his third day at home in his sweatpants and plaid bathrobe padding about, watching too much television, and making Anna and Emma wonder if he had completely lost his marbles.

All he would say to them was, "Something has happened, and as soon as I sort it out, I'll tell you."

"Make it sooner rather than later, sonny," Emma said, "because you're trespassing on my territory. I'm the one who wears the bathrobe around here."

"Am I crazy, or do you hear camera shutters going off outside the house?"

"You are crazy," she said. "Next question."

Anna, who was getting ready to go to work, had a different diagnosis. "You're going through the inevitable pains of the creative process. I recognize that's what's going on inside, A.B. You're gestating, preparing to write another novel."

"No one does any gestating in this house unless I say so," said Emma.

"I'm not feeling very well."

"Poor baby. Am I familiar with the creative writing process, or am I not? Just let it wash over you and through you, honey, and that next great book will surface for sure."

"What was the last great book?"

"Writers don't always know what's happening to them, Emma."

"That's for sure," said Konig.

"Well, A.B., I have confidence in you. And at the appropriate time you will tell me what's percolating."

Konig opened his mouth and was about to try to tell her, but what came out was: "Would you mind, on your way to work, stopping off at my office to feed Norman?"

"Must I?"

"You know the routine. Like me, he's not very demanding."

"Is that so?"

However, when she relented and agreed to go to the building to feed the mouse, Konig's relief was enormous.

While she was away, he went over and over again anything he might have done to draw the attention of the Executive Branch: He had had a Palestinian friend in college whom he now emailed happy birthday; he'd been doing this for a dozen years or so; was a dangerous pattern being detected here by the National Security monitoring apparatus? Was his email being watched? He'd occupied a building in college; in March 2003 he had demonstrated against the deployment to Iraq, had been arrested and let go and had appeared at a hearing, and charges had been dropped. That had happened to thousands of others, but were they being summoned to the White House in limos?

His soul-searching tired him and, along with Emma, he went back to bed and slept most of the morning. He was feeling much better by early afternoon when Anna returned home. She was very talkative and said things that at first made no sense to Konig but, once he understood them, he began again to feel his confusion and anxiety reignited.

"I went over to feed the mouse, and not only is your office vacuumed, A.B., for the first time in living memory, but those thoughtful secretaries—"

"—Paralegals, Sharon and Sandra."

"Well, they saw me when I entered, and they said that at Cheever and Bell's suggestion, they had also bought plants for your basement, so the place is now full of lilies and jasmine, and what not. And they all hoped we would not mind."

"Amazing," Konig said.

"And get this. Before I left, Cheever came out, introduced himself to me—I mean maybe I had stumbled into him years ago, or at the restaurant where I served him—but, A.B., get this: He sat me down in his office. Bell came in, and they offered me a glass of wine. 'Shiraz or pinot noir?' I chose the shiraz and it was very good. Then they said how pleased they were with you being a tenant, and they wanted to get to know *us* socially. Socially. I thought to myself, where does this come from?"

"That's a good thought to have."

"And then—this is the beauty part, A.B.—they said they knew I was a writer too, like you, but a poet. They said they had taken a new interest in poetry."

"Cheever has taken a break from his rapacious real estate transactions to take an interest in poetry?"

"That's right, honey. Both of them have suddenly taken an interest in verse. Close your jaws, A.B. You look like a crocodile. I'm just reporting. Listen, art is art. Do you think lawyers should, as a class, be denied access to literature? If a man expresses an interest in my poetry, I don't say, 'What do you do for a living?' I say, 'I'm flattered.' I say, 'Thank you from the bottom of my heart, and that's no cliché.' How could I refuse?"

"Refuse what?"

"Well, Cheever asked if I happened to have some of my work with me, on me. And since I did have three or four new poems in an envelope that I was taking to the post office for mailing, he asked to see them. He called Bell in, and they read the poems together."

"Now wait a second. These were your poems?"

"I just said so, didn't I?

"Yes, I mean your usual stuff. In your usual, your inimitable style?"

"Of course, A.B. So they read them over and then asked if they could read one aloud, especially if I had anything very new. And I said...well, here's one that I haven't even yet shown to my husband." Then Anna recited it:

Frog not dog and the monument
Seeks its depth reflected in the sky
Yelp the voice of the people
Cry and do and create the Flood

"After they heard that one –I guess I was a little embarrassed but it was beginning to feel good too—then, get this, they asked if I would give them permission to make copies. Why? They said so they could enjoy the poems, study them over at home, savoring them, sharing the pieces with their families. Isn't that astonishing?"

"Home with their families?"

"Uh huh. I haven't been so flattered…since I don't know when. Now, what's wrong, A.B? You suddenly look a little piqued." She tickled him. "Your gills gone green? You're not envious, are you?"

"It's a full-court press," Konig moaned.

"I don't do sports metaphors. What are you talking about?"

"Anna," Konig said. "I hope you won't be disappointed when I tell you this. But what's made me nuts these last days isn't artistic inspiration. Cheever and Bell's appointment—you remember when they asked to see me?—" she nodded—"they wanted to take me to see the President."

"Of what?"

"The United States of America."

Anna's pretty lips opened slightly into an "Oh" of amazement. "And you didn't go? Maybe you should have gone. Why didn't you tell us!"

"I freaked. I thought they have something terrible on me in my past, most of which, as you know, I can't remember. Maybe in a marijuana haze, I had done something or said something really bad, and now they were coming to haul me off. I confess I have been thinking and acting a little irrationally. But I mean, what could the President of the United States want with me?"

"Why didn't you ask Cheever and Bell?"

"They didn't seem to know either. They were trying to act as if they did, but I could see they were as in the dark as I was. It was suddenly *The Castle*. Kafka had landed. So I said, 'No thank you,' and ran home."

"Oh, my," Anna said.

"And now they want to read your poetry."

"Well, Cheever and Bell do, yes."

"Don't take this the wrong way," he said to her, "but it's possible these things are connected. Quite possible."

"What do you mean 'connected'?" she said with a defensiveness that surprised him. "Maybe they just like my work…maybe…but, no, there you go again ruining the whole thing."

"Cheever and Bell are all prose all the time," Konig said. "They know nothing about poetry, Anna. In fact, they're averse to verse if you ask me."

"No one's asking you, A.B. Maybe their ignorance, if that's what you call it, is precisely what makes them open to my new narrative strategies. To the freshness of my vision, to my through-line that's both invisible but also everywhere like the skein of life itself."

"Huh?"

"That's what they said."

"Who?"

"Cheever and Bell."

"They said 'huh' or the 'freshness' and 'skein' stuff?"

"Do I have to repeat everything? Are we living in couplets here, A.B.? Maybe they like my work simply because it's good? It's about time something nice happened , for at least one of us. It's been a long time between drinks around here."

"Okay, okay," he said, with a sudden supplicating nervousness, because he detected the first shiny oval of tears welling in Anna's big eyes. Her crying always unmoored Konig and made his equanimity, when it blessed him with its occasional visits, fragile as a bubble.

"Maybe I underestimated them, after all."

"I think they loved my 'Yelp,' honey. Honestly!"

"That's right," he said, sheepishly. "I'm sure they did."

"I feel energized to work now. And, A.B., I think you should get in touch with the President and see what he has in mind for you. What's it hurt to talk to him? Just calm down, shower, shave, and, you know, drop by the White House."

"It doesn't quite work like that."

"You always think the worst of people and things, always suspicious that some kind of plot is afoot. Both you and Emma."

Konig put his hands on Anna's shoulders and emphatically squared her to him: "Promise you won't mention a word of this to Emma. You know what she thinks of the President. She spits over her shoulder at the mention of his name. If she got an inkling I was asked to the White House, well, you have no idea what could be unleashed. She is a violent human being, Anna, and only your kindness, and her decrepitude, keep her under control."

"Oh, stop."

"If she thought I was going to set foot in the office of the Imperial President…"

"Come off it, A.B. And don't look around so furtively. She's upstairs. Asleep. I'll tell her you're going to the dry cleaners."

"That's good, " Konig said as he withdrew a large handkerchief from the pocket of his robe and wiped droplets of sweat from his forehead.

"Very good," she said, indulgently. Anna was already sitting down at the desk, arranging her pad and three pens, each of a different color, red, green, and blue. "Now leave me alone to do some work. Get showered and dressed to meet the President. And don't worry about Emma, will you?"

"I'll see. I guess it can't hurt."

"Thattaboy."

"What about Norman?" Konig suddenly remembered. "Did you get down there to feed him?"

"Sorry, A.B.," she said. "I got caught up in the poetry."

"Sure," he said. "I understand. What's the starvation of my assistant compared to the advance of poetry? What's the life of one tiny mouse add up to in the large scheme of the universe?"

"I like that," Anna said. "A mouse, a universe. A search for the universal house. No matter how small. What's a better word for 'small'?"

A mouse, a life, largeness
Not included
Laws, of course, plus pause
And paws yet
Just when you think,
Caesar Salad
Santa Claus, trips
A lightness in the air
Mistake aside our friend
Trap death oops

Check please

As Konig dragged himself out of the room and down the hall, he could still hear Anna working, composing her lines in the air.

Nine

"A.B. Konig," said the President of the United States, "how glad I am finally to make the acquaintance of the author of *Vengeance Valley Days*. Let me shake that talented hand of yours."

Konig now noticed, as the President rose and stood in front of his high-backed chair, that he appeared to be wearing running shorts.

"I sure hope you don't mind my informality."

"You should take it as a high compliment," said Kove.

The advisor now turned to his ghostwriter candidate. "The agenda has shifted, Mr. Konig. All this talk of, excuse me, Mr. President, for using the words—censure, impeachment, all the hearings, this is the realm of past-dwellers, of nitpickers, of small-minded men who don't have their eye on the country's future. We're concerned with the bigger picture, the longer view. In short, the presidential legacy. And that's why you're here with us today."

Konig was so struck by the President's unexpected, unaffected, and even goofy manner that he, momentarily, forgot that he was there to make an expostulation of his own, a few words of refusal and protest, respectful but firm: How can I possibly, Mr. President, given who I am, spiritually and politically, my background and values, sir, how could I ghostwrite a book for you? I'm flattered, of course, but there can be only one answer.

Then he would say his thanks-but-no-thanks and go home. Yet he found himself lingering, transfixed, even oddly and suddenly tempted.

"Our western novel project? Mr. Konig?" said Raymond Kove. "You seem to be daydreaming there. I trust we have your full attention."

Then the President placed his hands thoughtfully in his lap and said. "We have had terrific fun, Raymond and I, comin' up with titles for the book. *Ridin' to Riyadh. From Baghdad to Biloxi.* What are some of the others, Raymond?"

"*Mohammed of the Big Muddy, Gunfight at Sultan Creek.*"

"Clever," said Konig.

"We thought you'd like 'em," said the President with a clap of his hands.

"The title," said Kove, "should, of course, reflect the whole book, Mr. Konig, and its various themes, which have to be completely respectful of our Muslim brothers—the good, law-abiding ones, that is—and particularly those that reside in legacy-sensitive states."

"I'm thinkin' California, Texas, Michigan," said the President.

"Some scenes, yes, set in Michigan would be a good idea," added Kove.

"I've never heard of a western set in Michigan," said Konig.

"No," said Kove. "On the other hand, whoever thought most of the population of Dearborn would be Muslim? Or a rookie congressman would want to take his oath on the Koran? Mr. Konig, if the President has an intuition, it's just possible it could be done. Are you on board?"

Just then the door to the Oval Office flew open and Lenore George came in. The First Lady, a tall woman, in sensible square pumps, traversed in three long strides the blue carpet with its great woven seal of the United States. "Sorry to interrupt, gentlemen, but here are your trousers, Mr. President."

The three men stood up.

"Honey, let me introduce A.B. Konig, our favorite author."

She handed the President his pants with an exasperated fling of her arm, and then, towering over Konig, shook his hand. "A great pleasure, Mr. Konig."

"Lenore, tell him how much you like his books."

"Well," the First Lady said with a daggerish look toward her husband, "I felt you covered the territory, the story, very well, but without calling attention to it in any way that could be considered obtrusive. What I'm trying to say is how subtly you made the point about the vanity of power and fame. It puts me in mind of that African proverb you also somehow worked into the book—it's one of my favorite sections and I just can't remember the page number now –I hope you forgive me: 'One is born, one dies, the grass grows.'"

"I really said all that?"

"I'm only one reader, but, all I can say is, thank you, Mr. Konig, for a terrific and moving read." At the door, as she left, she added, "I think you will
be the perfect writer to secure Brewster's legacy."

"I'm flattered," said Konig, "but there are a million writers. What'd I do?
What's the real reason you asked me here?"

But before a presidential reply was forthcoming, Konig tamed his qua-
vering voice and organized the words he had prepared, and now sent them
out: "When you obviously know, when Cheever and Bell have told you who
I am, politically, why would I want to help you advance your legacy, sir, and
your party's? I oppose what you are doing, sir, respectfully. I oppose what you
are doing domestically, internationally, intergalactically, and, frankly, the
only thing I approve of is how your wife sews your pants for you. That was
very touching."

"Obviously, Mr. Konig," Kove proceeded, "we have considered other less
politically handicapped authors. Also as a ghostwriter, you surely are aware
that you are not quite top of the line."

"Watch how you phrase that, Raymond."

"What I'm trying to say is that, as the First Lady and the President have
made abundantly clear, you are, to them, not only a first choice, you are,
well, more than a writer, more than a ghostwriter. You are—"

"—You are exceptional to us, A.B.," the President interposed. "Your
words send us. Your situations, the way you always have the varmints fightin'
back, tooth and nail, like in that tunnel scene, and you like the bad guys
enough to respect 'em as fighters, to respect their skills and their devil-may-
care recklessness and love of speed, but we also know that their values are in
the toilet, they are evil, or close to it, and when you kill 'em off, there is no
doubt, absolutely no doubt in the reader's mind that they deserve to die.
And that in their cases, dyin' is good, and their rottin' flesh and blood will
make the farmer's crops grow, and good will rise from the annihilation of
evil. Those are the values we want in my book."

"Amen, Mr. President," said Kove. "That took my breath away."

"Oh don't be such a sycophant, R.K.. A.B. can see right through that.
He's a novelist."

"I'm really flattered, Mr. President, as I've said, but the problem is...I'm
glad your party lost the election, and as to your legacy, sir," Konig stam-

mered—he heard the shy timbre of his voice, but it didn't stop him—"I think you should stay in history's doghouse for at least several generations. Surely you know that. So here's what I can't figure: Even if I took the assignment—and, yes, absolutely, you know I need the money—how can you be sure I would produce the product you want? If I were you, Mr. President, I wouldn't trust me, or hire me."

"Is this a stand-up guy or what?" said the President. "That's exactly the kind of straight-talkin' integrity you give to your characters. That's why we want you, baby!"

"Absolutely," said Kove.

"The President wants to work on this book with you, and only you. Somehow, some way he will find time from the public's business to become a true collaborator with you."

"That is, A.B., if you'll let me. It would be an honor."

"It's not often," Kove sucked in his gut and spoke with gravitas, "that the President tells a dead-end ghostwriter he'd be honored to work with him. So we thought," added the advisor, "that once we explained the project in this context, you would, despite our political differences, consider it. You'll have another published volume to add to your shelf of masterpieces, and a nice piece of change in the bank, so what's to lose?"

"My conscience, Mr. President."

"Oh, that. Tell this lucky ghostwriter what more we're willin' to throw in to sweeten the pie."

"The President is prepared...will give you permission, Mr. Konig, to write a book about the writing of this book. You know, the insider's story. You're sure you don't mind, Mr. President?"

"No, I guess we don't, Raymond," the President said with a sudden sour look in his eye. *Tales of the Presidential Ghostwriter.* Somethin' like that. Sure. I guess."

"You'd really let me do that? Write an exposé of the process?"

"Hell, sure," said the President. "Tales and confessions of the presidential ghostwriter. Sure, go on. If that's what it takes to snag your services, you can be takin' notes on everything you see here."

"A two-book deal?" said a dumbfounded Konig. "It's been a long time since that's happened to me."

"Nineteen years, three months ago, precisely," said Kove, with a glance at his clipboard. "And it was canceled when the editor changed houses. So will you at least consider our proposal?" asked Kove, as they walked Konig to the door.

"Was that a yes or a no?" the President said.

"I believe that was the sound of my conscience, devouring itself," Konig heard himself saying.

"Raymond, did you hear that phrase? 'Devourin' conscience.' The juices are already flowin,' A.B. Why couldn't our hero have a conscience problem, say, just like yours? Lenore says the best authors write from what they really know deep down in their heart, and you obviously know conscious problems when you see 'em. So there you go. The hero has to do whatever it takes, and some of it doesn't go down so smooth with his conscience, but we'll work the details out later. But then maybe he meets a beautiful Muslim lady?"

"Terrific, Mr. President," said Kove. "The numbers dictate that we make her the beautiful daughter of a mixed Sunni and Shiite marriage."

"Right," the President ran on with bubbling enthusiasm. "How's about her bein' the daughter of a heroic but recently dead small family farmer or, better yet, factory owner? Say, I'm enjoyin' this. Still, moved as I am, I think we've got to wrap it up. What haven't we talked about?"

"The fee," said Kove.

"Ah, filthy lucre, moolah. Bring it on. Unless, of course, A.B. would consider doing this as a free-will act of patriotism? Of course not! Raymond?"

"The proposed fee is," Kove read from the clipboard, "for the work discussed…Let me see, yes, the Brewster George Presidential Legacy Committee is prepared, yes, here it is, $250,000. Will that be suitable?"

"A quarter of a million dollars to ghostwrite your book?"

"What? Not enough?" asked the President. "What could we throw in, Raymond? We could provide you the limo each day you come here, along with those two boobs we're workin' with. They can chauffeur you back and forth. You can be…like the C.E.O. of ghostwriters, Konig. Back and forth in the limo, and we'll give you a police escort too. What color you want your oscillatin' lights to be? Just say the word."

"I'm flattered again, but I'm not negotiating. I just don't think…"

Kove and the President exchanged a glance. "We could go higher, if we had to," Kove said. "We know you're an honorable man, Mr. Konig. Still we've checked the industry standards; our quotation seems right in there, solid and reasonably positioned—actually on the higher end."

"At first blush," Konig stammered, "very reasonable."

"Excellent," said the President. "I'm psyched."

"Whoa," said Konig.

"'Whoa!' Catch the horse talk?" the President winked at Kove. "The man is already in the saddle with us."

"We haven't made any deal, Mr. President."

"Of course not, A.B. We are just discussin'."

"Now, then," Kove said, "let me say how very nice it was of you to spend this time with us, Mr. Konig."

"On behalf of the People of the United States and the Presidential Legacy Committee, please accept our gratitude," said the President, "and a big hug."

The President then reached down and pulled Konig into an embrace that made the ghostwriter suddenly aware of how many ribs he possessed. "That's a dose of my very special 1600 Pennsylvania Avenue affection."

"Thank you, Mr. President," Konig said. "But at the risk of being ungrateful, for the record, I have not said yes."

"Where I come from, A.B., a 'not-yes' is a far cry from 'no.'"

Pulling out his card from his suit pocket, Kove said, "This is my direct line. When you come to your decision, call me."

"Or you can even call me direct, too," said the President. "Raymond here will give you my cell."

"Do you realize, Mr. Konig, how few people have the President's direct line?"

"That's right," added the President. "And I promise if it's you callin', A.B., I'll always answer and put even another prez or PM I'm talkin' to on hold. Right, Raymond?"

"On hold? Noted, sir."

They had by now, on their way to the exit, walked past the rigidly eyes-forward military guards, and they were quickly out in the Oval Office corridor. The President and Konig shook hands one more time; the President's grip was vice-like, which Konig understood to be the handshaking style of weak men.

"I know your head will be buzzin' with all kinds of things when you leave here," said the President. "For the moment all I ask is that you remember this: The White House might be the most powerful address in the galaxy. Still, when you find somebody you really like, the light is always lit, the latch is always out, the…What I'm trying to say, A.B. is: *Mi casa blanca es su casa blanca.*"

"Mr. President, you can use that in the western," Kove said happily. "It will be *mucho bueno* for the Hispanics. Now here," he went on, handing Konig a handsome brown Stetson. "We know your size, of course."

As he walked on the thick silent carpet, Konig heard Kove's voice behind him exclaiming, "It has legs, Mr. President." Kove was obviously deliberately speaking loud enough so the ghostwriter might hear. "We could launch the phrase in the novel, and then it could be usable for the whole legacy campaign and beyond into history. I can already see it on display in the library. Yes. Everyone, come on down to the White House because—"

"—*Mi casa blanca es su casa blanca,*" the President said gleefully as Konig moved down the hallway, this section lined with peering portraits of the presidents. The ghostwriter felt suddenly scrutinized by all of the past presidential eyes, and even a little haunted. As he now waited and stared at the illuminated numbers on the panel of the elevator ascending to open to him, Konig felt the way he imagined a deer feels crossing the road and becomes suddenly frozen by oncoming headlamps of a car about to strike him.

"Don't be scarce now, A.B."

Ten

"I have never seen you look so cute," Anna said that night as they all three were leaning over the Scrabble board and Konig was modeling the Stetson President George had given him. He kept on taking it nervously on and off, massaging the leather, and repositioning it on his head.

"Ponytail's in the way."

"Chop it off," Emma said absently.

"Not on your life," said Anna as she studied the board.

"Chop off some of that brain while you're at it," grumbled Emma.

"Come on now. You said you'd be nice."

Emma stretched herself over Anna's letter holder. "Use that blank letter there, and here's what you can do: Spell a four-letter word that begins with 'f' and ends in 'l' and looks exactly like your husband looks in that Texas cowboy hat."

"I got it!" she said with feigned excitement. "F- o- o-l. Happy now?"

"That's right, honey. And he's in danger of worse. He'll be a seven-letter word beginning with 't' and ending in 'r' if—"

"—A traitor to what, Emma? I'm not even a Democrat any more. I'm an independent. Anyway, I said no and gave the President an earful."

"Well, that's something," Emma said. "Still, I smell a rat."

Konig sighed, and then extended his arms, palms up as if beseeching some forgiveness from somewhere, anywhere. "I confess I liked the guy. Shoot me, but I did, sort of. That's the odd part that I never expected."

"What did he say?" Emma stood up to her full height and looked down at her great-nephew.

"Watch the blood pressure," said Anna.

"All I'm saying is I don't find him the complete monster everybody expects. Sorry to disappoint."

"I don't care if I pop every capillary that's left in my body but you are not going to do this project. He's a war-wager and a warmonger, and he's spying on us. He is making more enemies for us than we can shake a stick at. He ignores the voices of the people, including his own experts. He's the great liar and bamboozler. I've seen it before, believe me. Didn't we tell McKinley to watch that little twerp of a secretary of the navy of his, Teddy Roosevelt? Why, all that little man wanted were battleships to play with and a chance to cowboy it up and down San Juan Hill. Didn't we demonstrate, and shout, and..." Emma forgot where she was, but not for long. "And didn't we demonstrate in front of Hearst's office, you at my knee, boy!"

"Neither of us was born yet, Emma. And you know it."

"Show me what you know and what I taught you! That's my point."

"I merely said he was all right in a general, human sort of way. He's in way over his head, tryin', I mean try*ing* to act as if he knows what he's doing. I feel for that, I guess, but of course, I'm not going to work for them."

"On the other hand," said Anna. "A quarter of a million dollars?"

"Blood money! That's about what it costs to run that war for about the next half hour."

"The blood money will fix the roof, Auntie," said Anna. "And the plumbing too. A.B. wouldn't have to ghost dentist's autobiographies. Instead he could write the novel of his dreams."

"This is only making my head ache worse," Konig murmured.

"If you both wrote about working people earning a decent wage like I told you and the struggle of the masses for a decent life and health insurance, and how none of the sons of privilege in that Congress are dying over in Iraq, poems like my cousin Emma Lazarus would write about a Statue of Liberty today that can't hold the torch out anymore because she's back from Iraq and is a double amputee, *that*—instead of those inane pretty words you write, young lady—that would solve your problems."

"I do not write 'inane' verse, Emma. You don't understand the subtext."

"Subtext *drek*. You shape up, girl."

"Enough, Auntie," said Konig. "Blood money's everywhere. You don't want to be complicit, then don't answer your phone."

"I was proud when you told me you didn't have a phone any more," she said.

"Yet you conveniently forgot the reason. I don't have one because I can't afford it."

"You're being tempted, I can sense it, and this wife of yours is no help."

"Auntie, it just isn't every day the President of the United States fawns all over A.B."

"The devil is after you, sonny."

"I thought you were a card-carrying atheist."

"When are we going to see an opportunity like this again? I know it's heretical for us to be thinking this way, Emma," Anna said, "but consider Paramahansa. If A.B. turns his back on this offer, aren't we going to have to evict him and get a legitimate, paying tenant pretty soon? The bills aren't just going to disappear."

Slamming her letters resolutely down on the board, Emma declared, "We are doing all right. There will be no evicting on these premises! Even though the order of nature is reversed around here and you take from me, have I asked you for funds? Who's complaining, you spoiled creatures, you!"

"All right," Anna cried. "Enough!"

"You're counting money inside your pony-tailed little head. I hear rustling."

"That's the wind, Auntie."

"Does either of you remember the Haymarket labor riots of '86. That's 1886."

"Sure we remember it," said Konig. "Like yesterday."

"Blah blah. Indulge me. You think I'm on the verge of incoherence, but I know my history, A.B. Even though I may not always have it in the right order, there are lessons. How do you know that the quarter million the imperialists are dangling in front of you might not just tip the balance?"

"What balance? What are you talking about?"

"The balance of history. The workers' riots, then come the revolution. And when it comes, honey, I want you, I want *my* descendants to be on the right side of history."

"Lord, save me from Emma Lazarus, Emma Goldman, and Emma Konig," the ghostwriter intoned."

Anna, who had gone to the kitchen, returned now with three Red Dogs and two glasses; Emma always drank hers straight from the can.

"Auntie," she said, "doesn't it really come down to A.B.'s finally getting a chance? I'm only his wife and you're his blood relative, but why begrudge his getting a little break?"

"*Break* his head," Emma mumbled. "And yours too. You do know that man, Brewster George, is not really President of these United States? He's the Exaggerator-Manipulator-Liar-in-Chief. The Supreme Court installed him, illegally. Let these Democrats kick him out, or it's third party time."

"Exactly what I said to him," Konig whispered. "More or less."

"You did?" Anna said.

"I did, and lived to tell about it."

"What's this 'more or less'?"

"Not your exact words is all. The gist. I told him the gist."

"Piss on your gist, A.B. You caved."

"I did not. Here. I happen to have his direct number." Konig reached, not without a little panache, for the card, which he had been keeping in the hatband of the Stetson. He placed it at the very center of the Scrabble board. "Emma, you want to call the President? Give him a piece of your mind? Go ahead. No more flapping your gums in the breeze as the likes of us do. No more preaching to the converted. That number is direct to the devil himself. Use my name and he'll interrupt the most important international communications to talk to you, Emma, if you say A.B. Konig sent me. That's right."

"Wow, A.B.," said Anna.

"Oh, and reverse the charges," Konig added. The usual chatter ceased; the cone of yellow light that fell between the shaded fixture and the Scrabble board suddenly flickered as if a storm were just arriving. "Cat got your tongue?"

Emma's narrow face twitched slightly. "One of these days I *will* give him a piece of my mind. You'll see." Then she stuck out her tongue at Konig.

"All right, Emma," Anna said as she brushed hair from over the old woman's eye. "A.B.'s had his fun. Let's all just sleep on this."

"What good is *talking* to the alleged President anyway?" Emma said as they stood up. "Sure I'd enjoy it, but you confront power with power and with a plan, not my big mouth. It's you he wants, numbskull, not me, you embarrassment to your parents, may they rest in peace in Tampa."

"They're buried in Fort Myers," said Konig.

"The point is your father didn't raise you to be a turncoat."

Konig put on the Stetson once again and tipped it down over his face.

"It's you I'm talking to, sonny boy," Emma said as she swiped her arm around and knocked the hat to the floor. "I thought your head was screwed on a little tighter so that it wouldn't be turned by whatever it is they pulled on you there, pomp and circumstance and puffery and blandishments. You just remember who you are."

"A ghostwriter, Aunt Emma, a poor middle-aged ghostwriter who still has to borrow from his great-aunt."

"And none of us has any health insurance either," Anna added.

"So whose fault is that?" Emma said. "His Imperial George's, that's who. Oh, I know you're going to do this, so at least you might ask him to throw in a little health insurance along with your contract."

"You really mean that?" Konig was surprised by her capitulation. "In fact, I'm sure he'll insure all of us. No problem. Certainly for the duration of the job."

"Not just us! I mean let him insure the forty or fifty million working people who don't have any. How about you suggest *that* to him as a condition of your hire, and then you won't be such a sell-out!"

"I think she's serious, A.B."

"Oh, I am, I am, sonny boy. Hand me that card."

Eleven

No phone calls were made that night or the next day.

As Konig read in the morning papers how the President's approval numbers were plummeting still further, and, on succeeding pages, how Republican contenders in the upcoming election, even in traditionally strong areas like Idaho, Montana, the Dakotas, and Utah—good territory in which to set a gritty shoot-'em-up western—were always out of town when Brewster George dropped by for some barbecue, Konig figured his stock as a legacy western novel writer was only in danger of rising.

While he showered and shampooed, he tried to figure how to get a posse of Muslims out near the Rio Grande or just what target of justice they might be pursuing. As he shook out the rope of his ponytail, Konig began to wonder if, despite his best instincts and convictions, and the doom-saying disapproval of his Great-aunt Emma, he had already begun to work.

He dressed and put on a better shirt and tie than usual. If the President really meant what he said, then Raymond Kove would be pursuing him. Perhaps the offer, which Konig in his heart of hearts knew he should not and would not accept, might even be upped.

The day was bright, and the wind fine, as Konig made his way, as usual, on the bicycle to work. Yet it was difficult to sustain the illusion that everything was normal. To be wooed, to be the object of executive branch attention in this extraordinary manner, was an experience to which he could easily grow accustomed.

With suspicion and exhilaration duking it out within him, Konig angled across the avenue, turned into his street, dismounted from the bike, and gazed up. He was surprised to see Cheever and Bell on the steps, with Sharon and Sandra standing behind them like a greeting committee holding a small bouquet of carnations.

"Welcome," said the twins.

"What gives?"

"Mr. Konig," Cheever said, "We've taken the liberty of making some, well, rather significant lifestyle improvements in your basement suite. I trust you won't mind."

"My *suite?*" Konig, who did not like the things in his office disturbed, or even touched, especially where his mouse was concerned, glared at his landlords.

"Take Mr. Konig's vehicle, will you?" Cheever said to Bell, who promptly took Konig's bicycle as the ghostwriter accelerated past them to inspect the alleged improvements.

"Of course if you don't like what we've done, we can redo it to your specifications. Immediately."

Descending his steps, with Cheever and then Bell following, Konig beheld something he had never seen in the basement: actual bright sunlight.

"We took the liberty of punching a window through so you don't have to work in the darkness."

"But I like the darkness."

"Just a little touch up," said Cheever. "We think you'll get used to it."

Konig stepped carefully around his piles of books and manuscripts and milk crates of research, which had all been straightened, until he reached the rectangular window where now not only light poured through, but the light also fell on a display of half dozen plants, of different sizes and shapes, tendrils and leaves of begonia and hibiscus trellising up one side of the casement.

"As you see, we've moved out our old files, in case you need to expand, *should* you take on a new project," Bell said, with the hope of a supplicant in his voice.

"I haven't taken on anything new, gentlemen."

"*Should* you make that choice," Cheever repeated, "we wanted to give you additional working space."

"Okay, okay, gentlemen," said Konig. "Thank you very much. I get it."

"You, of course, are not obligated to pay us one dime for anything," said Cheever.

"Not a penny more for rent either," said Bell.

"Who *is* paying for this?"

Cheever and Bell smiled. "Let's put it this way. Although we might have, in the past, not treated you with the respect you deserve, Mr. Konig, lawyers can, well, sometimes, become rather insular."

"Come off it."

"We just appreciate you," Cheever went on, "in a new kind of light, as it were. A new way, a new perspective. And, by the way, we admire Mrs. Konig's verse inordinately."

"*Inordinately?* Gentlemen, really!"

At this instant one of the water pipes, which ran across the low-slung, dropped ceiling, gurgled and clanged. "We can reroute that too, Mr. Konig," said Bell.

"No plumbing repair is beyond the scope of our budgeting," Cheever added. "For what you are doing, for what you are about to do, maybe, if you so choose, and...Sharon, Sandra," he suddenly shouted up through the floorboards, "for god's sake will you please not use that facility at this time! How do you produce anything down here, Konig?"

"A good question."

"Ah, inspiration. That is how a writer is different from a lawyer," said Bell. "The imponderables, the invisible becomes visible...incidentally we tried to buy some of your books online, Mr. Konig, so that you might autograph them for us, but we couldn't locate any. I'm sure that situation will soon be rectified."

"You want my autograph?" Konig said, with a smile.

"What my colleague is trying to say," said Cheever, "is, well, it's as simple as, 'We are terrifically proud to have you in our basement.'"

Twelve

"Norman," Konig whispered several minutes after Cheever and Bell had finally ascended, leaving him in peace. "Norman, the coast is clear."

No answer.

"Norman, should I take this job?"

The mouse now hopped up from behind the thesaurus, which was propped against the leg of the computer table, and two little pinpoints of eyes appeared to be staring at Konig.

"Norman, do you see anything different about me?"

After pondering his answer for what Konig thought was an unusually long interval of exposure, the mouse fled. Konig tried to follow the faint rustlings of sound that marked the path across the floor of the office. Then suddenly Norman leaped and sailed above Konig's desk, landing delicately on it, and positioned himself, most appropriately, against the computer mouse. The crispy heel of a vegetable *quesadilla* that Konig had brought in and placed on the pad had done its job.

"The thing of it is," Konig confessed to the little mammal, "It's really counter to everything I've stood for, just like Emma says. She's absolutely right. On the other hand," he touched the mouse's front paw, "I am in a terrible rut. How else am I going to get out of it? It's so tempting. It all makes me feel like a little kid, doing a terrible thing, not getting caught, and getting a huge candy bar for it. Norman, give me your counsel, some sort of sign, and I'll gladly pay you for your time." He checked his vest pocket. "I have a square of Snickers left and a cheese cracker. You can have them both if you just advise me."

There was a deep quivering gray silence all around him, but the mouse did not stir. Upstairs Konig sensed the twins and Cheever and Bell tiptoeing about as if not to disturb his deliberations. Or, more likely, they were already spying on him.

"Legacy book or no book, the Republicans are going to lose in November," Konig reasoned with the mouse. "Whatever kind of western I come up with, could that possibly have an influence on the legacy? Kove is smart as they come, but on this score it seems preposterous. Doesn't it, Norman? Then why is Kove doing it? Could it be to give the President a kind of recreational release from the tension of the profiteering investigations and the war? Yes, I can see that, Norman. Sort of presidential writing therapy. And where's the harm in that?

"The harm is," Konig replied on behalf of the wise mouse, "George may personally escape it all—they always do—and the only way really to stick it to him will be to torpedo the legacy. So?

"You should have seen them, Norman. As for their genuinely liking my work, well, Kove and Brewster George certainly laid it on thick. They're probably still gloating over the success of their little dog and pony performance; so they thought.

"That part really should have pissed me off, kiddo, but it didn't. Norman? Say something, please." The recumbent mouse's head turned slightly and then quivered. However, Konig inferred just enough meaning from the gesture to go on.

"Right. We won't give them the satisfaction. On the other hand, yet again," Konig replayed his recollections of the meeting for the mouse, "there really was something about Brewster George that had surprised me. The man obviously wasn't much of a reader. Still, he somehow just *got* my books. Derived real pleasure from them, especially *Vengeance Valley Days*. That is no small thing, Norman. How many others read my work so carefully? Not even my own family. Yet at the White House?

"The President even quoted me. When's the last time you quoted me, Norman? You little pipsqueak, say something. Please!"

The mouse turned his eye to the ghostwriter and they sustained a long, mutually inquisitive stare. Occasionally—and it was rare indeed these days—when Konig had written a paragraph he was particularly proud of, and he tried it out on Norman, there might be a twitch of the whiskers on the left side of the angular face, a sign of mammalian comprehension. Yet now the mouse remained perfectly still.

The seductions of vanity aside, Konig had more than appreciated the bravura salesmanship of the President's and Kove's routine; whom else had he ever influenced with his words this way? Occasionally, over the up and down—mainly down—years of his writing career, Konig had received fan letters, but he could count them, on Norman's whiskers, ten or twelve at most. They were barely disguised self-serving corrections of some under-researched or arcane point. In one instance, someone did decide to return to high school after reading a short story of Konig's in which half a ham sandwich was wrapped in a G.E.D. diploma. Who could figure such things?

In the deep silence, while he fed the mouse a sliver of the Snickers, Konig listened hard for the promptings of his own wavering soul. God, was he really being tempted? Yet wouldn't Emma's blood pressure skyrocket to heart-attack level if he proceeded?

"Norman? You're good at hiding. What's wrong with hiding the whole thing from her the way you hide from me? Yes, Norman? No, Norman?" Konig whispered. "Twitch twice if it's a fool's errand. Come on, mouse. The free lunch is over. Work. Decide."

In the next instant the silence of the basement was shattered, and Konig was covering his ears against the pulsating sound of what he thought must be a fire engine or ambulance, with its loud blare just outside his new window. Wrong. The penetrating noise was coming from inside, near him. Very near. Konig leaped up, nearly knocking his head on the ceiling as he realized that what he was searching for was a telephone ringing at its loudest.

Norman suddenly rose on his hind quarters, and quivered as if the telephone sound waves were coursing right through him. Then he skittered across the desk, flew over a stapler and soared off the edge like a miniature high diver into the depths of books, papers, and junk on Konig's floor.

Suddenly Cheever and Bell were descending. "Answer it, please, Mr. Konig," Cheever said. "It could be—"

"—Who authorized you to connect my phone? Anyway, I can't find it."

"Mr. Konig," Cheever said as he stepped into the office, "The instrument is there, sitting on that green milk crate. It's a new cordless model. Grab it, for god's sake."

"I really was very happy without it."

"Mr. Konig!"

"It's either mute or shrieking. Nothing in between. I don't like telephones."

"Duly noted," said Bell.

"Will you!" Cheever snapped at his partner, and then caught himself. "If you prefer, Mr. Konig, we can yank your phone out later, but down here, sir, for this...interval, most reasonable people will conclude that you can't be expecting a call from the President of the United States, if you don't have a telephone to receive it."

Over the ringing, Konig shrieked, "I did not ask for this phone to be reconnected or for the window or for the cleanup."

"Will you please answer your phone, sir?" demanded Cheever.

"I was content with the way things were before."

"Mr. Konig, do you want the President of the United States to go into voicemail!"

"How do you know who it is?"

"Who else knows the line is working again?"

"It's on the sixth ring."

"I can count," said Konig.

"He's enjoying it," said Cheever. "Can't you see? He's taking pleasure in making the most powerful man in the world cool his heels."

"Seventh ring, Mr. Konig. This is a little unseemly. If you don't answer, permit me," said Cheever.

"Oh what the hell," said Konig. "Go ahead."

"Cheever, Bell, and Konig."

"Excuse me!" said Konig.

"Shhh," whispered Bell. "Sit, Mr. Konig. We dropped Einstein. You're a joke. No, that came out the wrong way. *Just* a joke."

"I see," said Cheever. "You don't say! That's wonderful. Yes, indeed. No, I haven't read the papers yet, but, absolutely, I will. Congratulations. Sure. It will be an honor, Mrs. Konig."

Before Konig could reach out and snatch the phone from his hand, Cheever had hung it up. "As you may have gathered, that wasn't the President, but a person even more important in your life, I dare say. Mrs. K."

"That rhymes," said Bell. "You're doing a lot more rhyming."

"Yes, well," Cheever said irritably. "She'll be over here shortly, and bearing a big surprise."

"What is going on?"

"If we tell you, Mr. Konig," Cheever said, as they maneuvered around the boxes and back up the steps, "then it won't be a surprise, will it?"

"She's going to divorce me?"

"That's not my impression," said Cheever.

"I have a lot of good contacts at family court, should Mrs. K. want to give you the old heave-ho," said Bell.

"That's not funny," Cheever said as he shooed Bell away, and sat himself down on the top steps. "You must shed this unuseful penchant for low expectations, subterranean self-esteem, this whole basement personality of yours, Mr. Konig. Why not embrace the light and your fortunate fate as a very powerful man of the moment, potentially? And I can assure you the news Mrs. Konig is conveying is good. Very good."

"I haven't decided. You know I haven't decided."

"Fine, fine, but I'm speaking as a friend. Yes, a sort of landlord, lawyer type-friend."

"And a friend of the administration."

"Of course, but we are human beings, Bell and I. Over our years of stumbling over you down here, do you think we've not also developed some human sympathy for you? I mean, Konig, long before these developments, you have meant something to us and to the girls. You're a human being. You're not a homeless man. You're the basement guy. That's how we would refer to you. The basement guy. With affection. You get my meaning, Mr. Konig?"

"I'm not sure. But go on."

"All right, then, why is it, sir, I get the impression that when good things happen to you, you see them as bad? When, speaking in the most general terms, of course, when opportunity knocks, even an opportunity that, for your profession, is about as big as it gets, you choose, or are apparently entertaining, the idea not only of shutting the door on it, but also of piling up the furniture barricading your door against these opportunities as if they were a horde of attackers. It's true we've improved your basement, but it would be mistaken for you to draw the conclusion that we think you should be a basement dweller for the rest of your days. Who would want to remain underground forever? A criminal perhaps. Wake up, Mr. Konig, enjoy your new sunlight, and breathe your new flowers. You should not consider yourself a prisoner down here. When your wife arrives, we are pleased for you to meet upstairs with her in the small conference room. In fact the girls are preparing it right now; we've cleared the decks, put off the other morning appointments to keep that room available for you any time, and on a moment's notice. You could meet up there, just you and Mrs. K. Confidentially, of course."

"I'm staying down here."

"It's as you like, sir. Good day, Mr. Konig. Call on us any time, and please check your messages."

Minutes later, preceded by a long plume of perfume—it was her going-out scent, which was a medley of new-mown hay, sandalwood, and bayberry—Anna Konig descended in a clatter of high heels, a rustling of stockings, and pages of newspaper.

"They published it, A.B. Look," she said as she dropped an overnight bag, purse, and computer case at the base of the ghostwriter's steps. "Where are you?"

"Here," he whispered.

"Where? I'm not staying if you're playing with that mouse again."

"Over here, and don't talk so loudly, please." Konig came halfway out of his hideaway beneath the steps.

"What are you doing, A.B.? Come out here. Turn on the light."

"No, you come back here. I haven't been able to find any wires or devices, but I'm sure they're recording us. FBI, CIA, NSA, TSA. All of them. Speak softly, and come back here, in the corner. The brick wall makes it hard for them to pick us up."

"Get a grip, A.B.," she said. "I am not going back there and getting this dress, which I haven't worn in a year, full of your cobwebs."

"There aren't any cobwebs, anymore. Shhhhh, Anna. The whole place is clean, and it's wired."

"You come out here and look at this paper. Take an interest. Ask at least which poem has been published."

"Okay," he said from the shadows. "Which poem?"

"They published 'Yelp,' and I can't tell you how excited I am."

"In Oink or Expletive?"

"Husband, look. Not in *Oink* and not in *Expletive*. You'll never guess where. In the *Wall Street Journal!*"

"Anna," he said, still in the shadows, "the *Wall Street Journal* does not publish poetry."

"They do now. You come out of there this instant and stop consorting with that mouse. Look at this!"

"All right," Konig said, "all right, but please keep it down." He emerged with gloved hands in one of which he held a pliers, and took the paper she extended to him, on which he shined the large industrial flashlight he held in the other. The full text of "Yelp" was not only printed right there on the op-ed page, all in italics, it also had its own oversized headline:

A New American Voice for a New American Era

"Is this the only copy, Anna? You know. Privately done. A joke."

"A.B., that is a very unkind remark. That is the *Wall Street Journal*, *WSJ*. And I happen to know it's also in the European and the Asian editions as well. The first time ever the *WSJ* has published poetry, and they chose me."

"My god, Anna!"

"No, not 'my god.' How about 'congratulations'? How about, 'way to go, my wife, my darling who has been working so hard, laboring so long in the vineyard, and finally a little harvest, and you go, 'my god.'"

"The voice, Anna. Please keep your voice down."

"Oh, I want to shout to the rooftops, A.B."

"But honey," he whispered, pulling her slowly into the shadows behind the steps, "you don't honestly believe—don't take this the wrong way—but the *Wall Street Journal?*"

"What's wrong with the *Wall Street Journal?*"

"They are just using you to get to me!"

"All I know is that they published the poem. I don't give an oink about *Oink* anymore. I'm tired of wasting my postage in trying to get my stuff into those tiny publications with a circulation of forty-three dreamers, forty of whom are also aspiring poets. They publish just their friends, and who reads them anyway, just like you're always saying. Admit it, A.B., you've always indulged me, thinking those little oinky aspirations of mine foolish as could be. But now, the big time. *The Journal*, and listen to you!"

"Stop saying that, will you? *The Journal*. Like you've been a valued contributor for years."

"You're all sour grapes, A.B. A newspaper read by gazillions of decision-makers and now they are reading my verse. 'Yelp' could affect the entire course of the economy, history, war, peace, everything. It's not quantifiable, of course, but then what is? All I know is that I'm out there, I'm communicating, finally. This is what I've been working for. You and Emma never tire of telling how the world really operates, the political and economic forces at play. So now the forces have propelled me. I refuse not to run with this."

"Anna. This conversation we are having is exactly what they want. This is hardball. This is what they do. I mean, if the President can get *The Wall Street Journal* to change the policy of its editorial pages and to publish 'Yelp,' is there any limit to the power? This is scary."

"A.B., you are disappointing me. You are descending into a paranoid Emma-esque view of the zeitgeist that a woman less patient than I would say is hardly more than a screen for your professional jealousy of your long-suffering wife's achievement. I propose this incredible literary breakthrough for me has nothing to do with you. It's entirely about the quality of the poems. No *quid pro quo*."

"What bullshit, Anna. And you know it."

"All right, A.B. Hardball. Let's just say that, theoretically, it is all about their getting to you through me. So, for your non-accepting of the assignment, they do this for me. Now, consider, if you were to accept, what would happen as a result of that? Today the *Journal,* tomorrow what? The Pulitzer Prize? Why don't we play this out for all it's worth and see where it carries us? I'm ready for an adventure. How about you?"

"But it's all so dishonest, honey. Are you so desperate?"

"Desperate is not the word I would choose. Interested, yes. Eager, yes. Desirous, yes. Aflame with ambition, also yes. And, frankly, you should have some of that too." She looked at her watch. "I've got a plane to catch now."

"Excuse me?"

"They didn't tell you?"

"Uh-oh."

"Hold your horses, A.B. I have an appointment up in New York at the…at the paper's editorial offices. Mr. Bell is going with me. And after that, guess what?"

"The Hague? You're going to read 'Yelp' at The Hague. No? The General Assembly of the United Nations? Maybe at an international conference on Iraq? No. For that occasion you'd have to read something called 'Help.' Have you written that one?"

"Behave yourself, A.B. I've been asked to read some verse at the board meeting of Tonoco Oil."

"My god."

"Smile, A.B. Please. I'm sick of seeing you down in the dumps, especially in this dump, and I've been waiting tables for too long. I'll bring you a plant from New York that makes good oxygen. This is it, honey. We are launched." She gave him a quick kiss, and then picked up her purse, computer, and traveling bag.

"When I work late, who's going to look in on Emma while you're away?"

"Honestly, A.B., I hope you *can't* get home because you're too busy working away down on Pennsylvania Avenue. Please, honey. Handle it. There's always Paramahansa. In fact I asked him already to look in on her."

"But," he felt himself grasping for words, any words, "what about Iraq and the Iran mess? Anna, please don't go. What about oil dependency?" He felt as long as he continued to talk, she'd stay there in his new basement, wouldn't leave him in mid-sentence, so he kept them coming. "Oil's the cause of it all. Doesn't any of that matter to you any more? Anna?" He may as well have been asking himself the same question. He *was* asking himself the same question. "That doesn't bother you any more?"

"I'm promoting poetry, A.B. And it's no sin. Poetry to economists, businessmen, stockholders, and oil companies. What can it hurt? A humanizing and civilizing influence on the warmongers, if you will. Find whatever language soothes your tormented soul. Oh, I love your torment, A.B. It makes you funny and who you are, but it's time. It's way over time. You find a way to make what they want you to write work for you too. You take the reins," she said, confidentially, "and you know where to find me."

"I do?"

"Waldorf Astoria, courtesy of—are you ready for this?—Tonoco Oil. Come on, make that little call, get your marching orders, and then take the shuttle up and we can celebrate, A.B. We can have that real honeymoon we never had."

"What do I tell Emma when she asks where you are going?"

"I know I sound cruel, A.B., but life is too short to spend any more time sitting around the Scrabble board hashing out whether WMD counts as a word. You're an imaginative writer. You tell her anything you want. She's sharp, still, she *is* a hundred years old, A.B. And, most of all, she really wants to believe in you."

Anna checked herself in her mirror, and climbed two more steps up. "Well, the starter gun is raised, the finger is squeezing the trigger, the…"

"Anna, don't."

"I love you," she said as she hoisted her bags over her powerful shoulders. "Remember. 'Yelp along with me/the best is yet to be.'"

"Anna! Anna."

She was up the last steps, two in a leap, and onto the landing where Konig, following, saw Bell take her by the arm and escort her into the waiting limo. That gesture had a paralyzing effect on him, and the ghostwriter could go no further. Only Anna's perfume lingered there for him on the steps, and in the basement, to which he now returned.

Thirteen

"In my country," Paramahansa was explaining to Emma as he served her and Konig a vegetarian pilaf dinner, "we have much that is at the same time both scenic and almost completely decrepit: falling-apart sea walls, broken bridges, severed highways that run up to a grove of picturesque cypresses and then suddenly dead end; even school buildings where sometimes the children of Brawada sit out in the open, always in a circle, which is the holy formation my countrymen prefer, and, alas, these days, often in a roofless classroom so that the sun and rain pour down on them and on our dedicated instructors. Yet as long as the beautiful little ones possess even a single book, a single chalk board, one dedicated teacher, or even one square meter of dry sand on which to teach geometry between the inundations that flood and bedevil our beloved atoll, no matter how forlorn, soggy, and in bad shape we are, the learning goes on. That is my country's commitment."

"That's all very moving, Ambassador," said Konig.

"I tell you this not to make the case for increased foreign aid for Brawada for you to pass on to your president, but to reassure you that in Miss Anna's absence, your beloved Great-Auntie has nothing to fear, not even fear itself. For just as all the members of my island nation know how to take care of decaying infrastructure, thus these lessons are passed along in our communal knowledge of the care of the elderly."

"Beautiful, Mr. Ambassador."

"And a pack of lies," said Emma. "Where is that girl?"

"I told you. She's shopping up in New York. With some of her girl-friends."

"What do they have up there that she can't buy here?"

"I couldn't tell you," Konig said. "She's shopping. I'm not a shopper."

"What do you make of this, Ambassador? In your diplomatic business, aren't you trained to spot bullshit?"

"We tend to accept that people are telling the truth, Miss Emma, unless proven otherwise."

"Just look at this puss," she said, reaching out her long thin arm and chucking Konig on the chin. "Look at that. That's all the proof you need. Something's fishy. You get this big offer to do that bloody man's bidding, God knows why, and then you refuse him. You refuse the President, as well you should. You do the honorable thing and you make me proud. Then your wife runs out on you? What gives?"

"Nothing gives, Emma. She's not run out on me. She is shopping."

"Oh, now I see. Did those bastards take her away from you? Are they threatening you? Are they using her to make you reconsider? Ah hah! Bingo. Eureka!"

"Miss Emma," said the Ambassador, "would you like more rice and pine-apple? And what do you think of it? It's the specialty of my poor country."

"Could use a little meat," she said, picking away at the brown heap on the plate before her. "Maybe that's why your people are so decrepit, your GDP's in the toilet, and you're not paying your dues or your rent to yours truly. Can't you throw in some goat or something?"

"Miss Emma," he said. "Add some salt."

"You guys are pulling the wool over, and I know it."

"I think it's time for me to carry you up to bed, Miss Emma," said the Ambassador.

"Don't put a Brawadan hand on me. Not tonight."

"Let me help you get ready," Konig said.

"Not you either. Suddenly I have some new-found strength." Emma rose to her full height. She steadied herself using the tabletop, and gave both Konig and Paramahansa a blistering look that Konig knew all too well. "Your lying's helped to arouse me, fellas. I'll just go up to my room by myself. It'll take a few eons, but, thank you, I can manage. And thank you, Ambassador, for the meal."

"It's the least a poor tenant can do."

As soon as Emma was out of earshot, Konig's irritability and the sense that he'd made a mistake in taking Paramahansa into his confidence got the better of him. "What's the idea of asking me to appeal to the President? That was a stupid move, Mr. Ambassador. That's what got her going. You make a lousy diplomat. I just might recommend to the President that your country recall you!"

"I have had many fears of being recalled, it is true. However, even recalling me requires funding to cover the airfare to bring me home, which the poor exchequer does not at this time possess. Please accept my apologies, Mr. Konig. Now and then I am the beneficiary of my nation's poverty. And I hope I remain your revered tenant and confidant. Do you want me to come up with another five or ten bucks?"

"Stop that, already."

"You are most upset. We can do some yoga perhaps?"

"No, thanks."

"Upward Dog, Sun Salutation, and then Downward Dog will relieve much of your tension."

"I'll pass."

"Then may you feel better, and praise Allah to the rooftops, they need serious repair. What will you do about your revered assignment for your president?"

"I'm still thinking. I'm figuring how. Just help me, you know, occupy Emma. Spend time with her. You don't have anything else to do since you're not being allowed into the General Assembly until you pay up."

"That is very sad, yet true."

"If I were you, I'd keep Allah off the rooftops. There's a good chance every time we yawn here, they're recording it at Langley. You don't want to be deported, do you?"

"Yes, yes. I mean no, no."

"Please take care of Emma like you do your beloved island, until I figure this thing out."

"From this day forth, she shall be my chief duty. I can take her to the zoo. Would she like to visit the birds of prey with me? Vultures are my favorite."

"I'm sure she would love it."

"'Let the wind gusts blow,' says one of my country's most notable proverbs. 'Yet will we harness them to our sails. Thus the fury will move us to our goal.' In other words, no problem, Mr. Konig."

"Whatever," Konig said. "Please feed her well. A lot of yoga. Keep her strong, even at her advanced age, just in case—"

"—in case of what, sir?"

"In case of nothing," Konig muttered. "I'm going to hit the sack too. Goodnight, Mr. Ambassador."

Fourteen

"Well, then, sir," Konig was saying, between short breaths, for even his many years of relatively strenuous bicycle riding were no preparation for President George's very rapid pace on the treadmill, "We start out with a general idea for the book. A vision."

"The ole vision thing. I like that. But first tell me, how's that machine? If you don't like it, we can send over to Interior for another."

"Treadmill's fine, Mr. President. It'll take some getting used to is all," Konig panted.

"A.B.? Let's up the pace."

"All right. At your mercy, Mr. President."

He ran on, accelerating vainly to keep pace with the President, his ponytail flopping from shoulder to shoulder, as he tried to keep a smile on his face, though his cheeks and forehead began to redden. Most of all he tried to stifle his doubts.

After a seven-fifteen mile, the President slowed down and talked to him: "A.B., I sense your tentativeness still, that the closer you get to fulfillin' your ghostwriter's destiny, which now coincides with my legacy, the more I sense you might be walkin' around, your head hung down low as if you were expectin' someone to chop it off."

"Uh, sort of, Mr. President."

"Good, so, listen up. I've come up with a way that's neither all or nothing, A.B. Take the job on provisionally. Contract to do a chapter at a time, and see how it feels. A kind of trial that lets you be my temporary probationary ghostwriter. That's what you'll be. That way you can play all the head games you need to with your values and your conscience and your Great-Auntie, and I can get started with my western because the people need to hear from me, this western needs to get written. How many you think we can sell, A.B.?"

"We haven't written a word yet, sir."

"My job's to think on the big picture, and I'm sensing that presidential legacy already.

"You're getting way ahead of yourself, Mr. President."

"Brewster."

"I can't."

"People say I don't have a vision, but I do, and I wanted to show you a little of it rarely seen by the public so as you can work it into my character. The compassionate visionary and the decider. And no contradiction between the two. That's me, keepin' it simple and straight for the people. But I got a callin' here, so spell it out, A.B., so you don't twist and satire things up, a callin' that goes deep, true, and clear as an underground Texas stream. You can take your polls and your study groups, and..."

"And what, sir?"

"And set them all aside, because there's only one thing I know how to do, and that's listen to the voice within and to surge ahead. I believe with perfect faith that one day Baghdad will be as safe as Baltimore. Heck, they may even take a liking to baseball and build them one of those vintage little stadiums. If so, I mean to go out there and throw the first pitch, even if I got to be leaning on my walker to do so. You should be there with me, A.B. I'll get you great seats. Only question is: first base or third base line? What do you say, pardner?"

"I don't know. I just don't—"

"—I'm throwin' a whole lot at you today, so what's that smart Hebrew head of yours makin' of it all, A.B.? Can you accept the job not only with the words you utter, but with love in your heart?"

"Love?" These surprising presidential intimations unsettled him. "Now I really don't know, Mr. President."

"It's not very manly of you, engagin' in all this ditherin'. You need some research help, is that it? I got this Iraq Study Group team that finished its job. I can lend 'em all to you if you want, though they're not good for a whole helluva lot if you want my opinion."

"I do my own research, Mr. President, but thanks."

"I understand, son."

"You do?"

"Yup. I really do. I'm lookin' at you in your deep brown Jewish eyes, and I like what I'm seein'."

"What do you see, Mr. President?"

"I see a boy who loves his wife, his granny or auntie or whoever she is, and a boy who loves his Jewish people and the democratic State of Israel too, as much as I do, and who's as scared of these Islamo-fascist lunatics as the next loyal American. You know it's our God's truth, A.B., that there's an army of terrorists, the worst sort of human imaginable. When I think of 'em, I can't help but feel that the Good Lord was nodding off when he created them. And they're out to kill you and to kill me, Jew and president of this great country alike. You and me, baby, in the same boat. They're not just out to do it, they're salivatin' to do it. So just step over that conscience or hesitation of yours, as if you were a kid and it's a crack in the sidewalk. That's what I see."

Konig blinked. "You see all that?"

"Uh huh. Just climb in the saddle with me. Presto-chango, you'll be the per diem probationary temporary presidential ghostwriter. That's my idea, that's the solution. Any time your moral crisis rises up and grabs at you with all those bad feelin's—and I been there, A.B., I know that feelin' of not being able to look yourself in the face in the morning, but, what the hey, it goes away if you give yourself a little wink—my point is that by this arrangement, you can quit anytime you want. No pressure. How's about it?"

"Gee, Mr. President," Konig said and then, inexplicably, the ghostwriter dropped his head into his hands, and began to weep.

"You're not some neutral bore of a writer, A.B., but a scribe who feels deeply," the President said as he released Konig from a withering embrace. "Take it from me, A.B. Hacks don't cry. You're the true article, temporary per diem ghostwriter, with a feminine side he's not ashamed of. Let's shake on it."

Konig saw the presidential hand nearing him, but hesitated. "I feel a little guilty, sir," he said, "accepting your hugs but still being leery of your hand."

"You're a piece of work, A. B. Konig."

"I'm touched, Mr. President. I mean I know what you're saying is a crock, sir, but I'm still touched, oddly touched. I cried, because I'm preparing to believe this is all on the up and up, when I'm fairly certain it's not."

"The important thing is to get your juices flowin' for the legacy book. Personally, I think we got a deal here. So where you at, A.B., coz my other duties call?"

"If I do it, I'll insist on secrecy."

"My middle name. A.B."

"You said compassion was your middle name."

"I have many, many middle names. Stick around, write well, and I'll tell you the others. And keep this under the Stetson as well: there's also a secret handshake."

Just then, the door to the Oval Office opened, and Raymond Kove entered, with a spare towel for the President. "Ah, Raymond, A.B. wants us to keep the western novel project a secret."

"Normally, of course, the ghostwriter is just that, a shadow. His name never appears on the book," Kove said. "So secret is the way it shall be for our per diem probationary temporary ghostwriting consultant."

"And no more limos sent for me either. In addition to being per diem, temporary, probationary, and consultatory, I also want to be green. I want to keep using my bicycle."

"That's real good cardio, A.B., but don't you waste a lot of precious time bikin' to work? I mean we've got a serious deadline launchin' my legacy express here, A.B.," said the President, with renewed seriousness as he toweled off. "Every time these nasty hearings get some Brewster-bashing headline, we want to be able to release, say, a chapter, serialized, from the book. Right, R.K.?"

"That's the way, Mr. President."

"The main point here is that my legacy's gonna last forever. That don't mean it should take forever to get written."

"I think while I bike, Mr. President. Just as you do while you run."

"Gotcha. No limos, no hoverin'. Bicycle only. Are you takin' this down, Raymond? These conditions?"

"Every word, sir. I would point out, however, that you're keeping your next appointment waiting."

"Who's that?"

"The North Korean delegation, Mr. President."

"Oh, them. They been makin' us wait for ten years, so what's ten more minutes? Heck, I got A.B. Konig here. Go brew some tea for the Buddha-heads."

"Tea coming right up. Yes, sir."

"Uh, oh. I see some more hesitation in your eyes, A.B. Now what else can the President do for you today so's we can get this little book goin'?"

"It's about my wife, sir."

"What about that beautiful cutie? We hear her career has taken off."

"Big time," said Raymond Kove.

"You know exactly what I'm talking about: *The Wall Street Journal*."

"She's not married to A.B. Konig for nothin'. She writes beautifully and deserves all the recognition in the world. Say, R.K., do Koreans like poetry?"

"I would think so."

"So, are you readin' me? Maybe we ask those guys out there about a Korean translation of Mrs. K's poetry."

"Sky's the limit, sir."

"Too much. Too much," said Konig.

"Now, now, A.B. I'll give you another hug if you want, although I'd like to save a couple for the Asians. They're so formal, and I don't do any bowin' except to my Lord, and my wife. It always gets to them. Now, don't begrudge your wife her success. This country supports the arts."

"No, no," Konig said."

"What are you mumbling about?"

"I guess I'm still a little stuck between a rock and a hard place. I'm sorry, Mr. President."

"No you're not. And even if you were, A.B., take it from me: there's a helluva lot of light between a rock and a hard place providin' you know where to look. Between a rock and a hard place there's commissions, hearings, study groups, and consultations until the cows come home. You can drive a truck between a rock and a hard place, A.B. What do you think politics is all about? It's just a question of knowin' the territory."

"That's very good, Mr. President," said Kove.

"Knowin' the territory, that's a catchy phrase, isn't it, A.B.? We could use that in our western."

"We could, sir. I think it's a reference to *The Music Man*," Konig said dolefully.

"That's not a western, is it?"

"That's a mid-western, Mr. President. It's about Iowa I think."

"How's the legacy doing in Iowa, Raymond?"

"Not bad," said the advisor. "Now, sir, may I make a few literary suggestions since you and Mr. Konig seem already to be launched on the project, in your own way?"

"Okay, A.B.?"

"On second thought, what about the Koreans, Mr. President?"

"I'll deal with the Koreans. Talk to us, R.K.. That's why the People employ you."

"What this story needs, sir, as I've been visualizing it, is the tracking down of evil characters who are threatening to blow up something big, something important for the country, like the Transcontinental Railroad. We need a kind of evil genius of a gang leader who somehow has the capacity to kidnap knights of the new American capitalism from the banks of the east, that is, forces that are threatening job creation back then, out to terrorize the railroad magnates and hold them for ransom. And they have access to the latest WMD of the time, say, dynamite and nitro. The ghostwriter can check the dates and the facts. Right, Konig?"

Konig's tongue, mouth, and voice surprised him by their apparently involuntary collaboration, sending out the word: "Absolutely."

"So, Mr. President, to counter these guys we then need a gang of cowboys, composed of good Muslims, and maybe a few Jews, but not too many, and this time they should be in proportion to the Jewish population at the time, in the 19th century, which was not too many."

"Are you takin' this in, A.B.?"

"Above all, Mr. President," Kove went on reading from his clipboarded notes, "we need to be led by a great posse commander, by someone quite like yourself, Mr. President, a handsome Christian knight-errant type of fellow, as we discussed, sir, in the guise of a cowboy who leads them through the states, planting legacy-bearing seeds, so to speak, of heroic deeds, and gathering members of a posse comitatus for the final battle and ultimate victory. Now, if that can take place, let's say, in a town named something like Armageddon, Michigan,—and perhaps in a corral but with a view of church in the background is the way I am picturing the final scenes unfolding, that would be very convenient, Mr. Konig."

"Whew," said the President, in a sweat of admiration. "Is that an assistant or what?"

"That's a tall order," Konig sighed.

"That's precisely why we chose the one and only author of *Vengeance Valley Days*, a writer who knows how to make his words kick butt."

A dozen or so sounds, which were taken by all for angry expletives in the Korean language, were suddenly floating through the doors of the Oval Office. The sweat, which had been pooling at the small of Konig's back, now began to make a little rivulet down into his briefs. He took a step backwards as the doors swung open, and a peeved First Lady stuck in her head. "I am sick and tired of bowing, smiling, and making excuses, Brewster. Please!"

"Say hello to A.B. Konig, honey. How do you say 'howdy' in North Korean?"

"Mr. Konig," she said with a polite if rigid nod to the ghostwriter. "Time, Brewster. Time."

"I think our meeting's concluding, Mr. Konig," said Kove. "I take it we have a yes? No? Yes, Mr. Konig? Or no?"

Feeling like a metronome, but without any music playing in the room, Konig looked back and forth between the First Advisor and the President. During the ensuing interval, he studied the treadmill, which was still moving on its silent rollers in the corner of the room. He noticed the speed with which the carpeted track circled around the turning cylinders. Should he accept? A single chapter seemed reasonable. A kind of experiment…trying it on. He felt dizzy, upended, he had been on the treadmill far too long. Had he stumbled while running on it, his toe, foot, his leg, then his torso, all of him, gradually might have been pulled down into the mechanism, flattened, and—well, that would be a solution. He didn't say no.

"Awright," Brewster George said, with the biggest presidential smile Konig had seen yet, "Shake this hand, A.B. Shake it now."

And Konig did.

Fifteen

The courageous Muslim cowboy, covered with dust, was riding hell for leather, across the saguaro-strewn desert. He was the lone human figure out there in that stark landscape, but he was not alone, for he was accompanied by dreams of justice and of glory. It was almost dark and he had only reached the top of the butte overlooking the New Mexico Territory.

Konig spent a half hour wondering if this opening was, well, too cinematic. Then another half hour pondering if he was too attached to the saguaro-strewn phrase. How many people will know it's a cactus he's talking about? If they don't, the whole effect is lost.

He slipped his glasses down the bridge of his nose and rubbed his tired eyes so deeply that he could feel the full concavity of his sockets; and the message from his skeleton was loud and clear: this project, barely begun, is already killing you. Still, he had shaken the presidential hand and he had to press on, and he began to revise in the knowledge that tagging the cowboy as a Muslim at the outset was not the way to go. There had to be something he did, some action, so that the reader, without having to be told, will, in a more engaging manner, infer his faith.

Then again, the antagonist, what would he look like? And how would he talk? Konig paced his silent office, picked up the *Washington Post*, replete with the latest bleak news, but, here, this headline spanning the front page immediately grabbed him: Saddam Hussein had been executed. Ah, a gift, Konig thought, for with Saddam now dead in real life, he could come back to life in fiction, in *this* very story he was launching. The evil one, pursued by our hero, whoever the hell he was, captured, escaped, captured, escaped, and captured again to do even worse depredations. Konig uttered a low, writerly "Aha," closed the paper, and returned to what he had written.

It was, however, a good stroke, Konig thought, to start neither with the evil one, nor with the Christian hero, but a loyal Muslim sidekick.

Which way was east? Pervez had lost his way, and now the courageous cowboy, covered with dust, was riding hell for leather, across the cactus-strewn desert. He was the lone human figure out there in that stark landscape, but he was not alone, for he was accompanied by dreams of justice and of glory.

If you were riding with Pervez and had a sharp eye, you might have discerned sticking out of the corner of his mottled saddle bag a book with strange cursive letters rarely, if ever, seen before in these parts.

It was almost dark when the cowboy on his Appaloosa reached the top of the butte overlooking the New Mexico Territory. Here he pulled up his horse, dismounted, calmed her with a practiced stroke of his callused hand across her long, sweaty face, withdrew a small carpet (decidedly not Navajo or Hopi), removed his well-worn boots, and then three times prostrated himself on the desert sand.

"Allah Akhbar, Allah Akhbar," he declaimed, but there was no call in return except the mournful cry of the hungry wolf and the cackle of the hyena, and the shake of the horse's reins.

The only question this effort provoked, Konig concluded, as he packed up his papers, was whether he should shoot himself in the office, or at home.

Perhaps if Norman had shown himself, Konig's writing progress might have been better. Or even if he had heard the reassuring rat-a-tat-tat of the twins' four high heels above, or the familiar whoosh of the old plumbing. However, with Bell in New York minding Anna, and Cheever mysteriously absent, it was as silent as a sepulcher throughout the building.

Konig rearranged boxes hoping to uncover Norman tanning himself beneath the corner lamp—yet it turned out to be only a folded up bicycle glove. Konig picked it up, and paced. He slid open and shut his new window, sharpened pencils, even cleaned the keyboard. He'd better come up with something soon. After all, his client was no longer a retired oral surgeon but the President of the United States.

Konig had promised to send Kove not only a draft of a chapter, but also a full outline, however preliminary, for the entire novel, with setting, plot, and brief character descriptions. This material was due, by email or fax— Konig checked his watch—one hour ago. Yet all he had was this meager beginning. Konig sat and sat, and nothing came out of him. What was there to do but go home, get some sleep, and try another day?

Feeling like a lamp unplugged, he left the office in the gathering darkness and pedaled toward home. The bicycle wobbled, and his progress was erratic, for his brain, distracted and divided against itself by the obligation he had taken on, was full of the interior monologues that accompanied his rides, only far more cacophonous and accusatory than usual. Why haven't you called me in two days, Anna? he asked her. I know there's a lot to see in New York, but, dammit, we've never gone forty hours in our whole marriage without speaking to each other. What? Am I your child? I have to check in every day? Grow up, A.B.

When he turned and angled steeply onto his street, Konig's helmet slipped off his head, but he let it dangle around his neck by the strap. Nooselike, it felt all too comfortable there. As he dismounted, hoisted the Schwinn onto his shoulder, and carried it up the stoop, Konig wondered if he had simply made a terrible mistake.

Although he tried to enter quickly and not look down at the basement, there was no avoiding the eager wave of Paramahansa, whose upper body was framed by the window, as if he had been waiting there for hours to ambush Konig. The ghostwriter paused, Paramahansa opened the door, and looked up at him expectantly from the steps below.

"Your revered Emma is resting nicely," he said. "I fed her a good dinner, with extra strips of goat meat as she requested. I discussed the news of the day with her, and put her to bed. Then the business of my country called."

"Mine too," said Konig distractedly. "Is she already asleep?"

"The excellent lady was a little tired. She asked about you, and, of course, Anna."

"But you know nothing. You played dumb?"

"As you Americans say, No problem."

"Please keep it that way."

"Did you, however, have a chance to discuss with your revered President the situation of my country? If Brawada were forgiven its debt, your rent could be paid. No problem."

"Listen," Konig white-lied, "I do not have a direct line to the President. And if I did, he's not going to listen to me about the problems on your atoll."

"It is too bad the world knows so little about us. We are one of the few countries where Christians and Buddhists share power in a deeply coopera- tive spirit with the Muslim majority.

"If it's such a religious paradise, Paramahansa, how come everything's falling apart there and you're always broke?"

"You ask such intelligent questions, good sir. My people do spend much time in interfaith dialogue. When one dialogues and meditates a great deal, the drains tend to get clogged. However, the positive side is we do not kill each other or even speak badly of each other. The atoll is indeed a mess. However, it is also a little sunken paradise, when the electricity works."

"Very touching," said Konig. He thought he could use a little paradise in his life right now, and a beer. "I'm only a writer, Paramahansa. You know that. Per diem, temporary ghost."

"Writers—as well as ghosts, I might add—are held in exceptional regard in Brawada. Perhaps you will come to visit some time to conduct a master workshop, or to be a writer-in-residence, once the immense pothole in our airport's single runway is repaired."

"It would be an honor."

"In the meantime, in light of my services, can you forgive my rent debt this month, sir? In its entirety?"

"Consider it forgiven, Paramahansa."

"May you have a peaceful night, good landlord." Then the Ambassador bowed deeply to Konig, who returned the gesture. Dog tired, he carried his bicycle inside, and entered the apartment.

He threw his briefcase onto the chair in the bedroom, whose silence exclaimed its emptiness without Anna. Resisting an impulse to rip open the folder with *Ridin' to Riyadh*, or whatever they were calling it, and to crumple the papers into a balled mess, Konig instead went into the kitchen, found an ale for himself and one for Emma, just in case he found her awake, and climbed wearily up to his great-aunt's bedroom.

Above her bed was a large framed poster proclaiming the innocence of Sacco and Vanzetti—a clenched fist of such straining and vein-popping power moving across the plane of the picture and coming right at you as you entered that Konig often wondered how Emma could sleep with all that vehemence going on just a foot or two above her head.

But sleeping was precisely what Emma was doing, and he thought such deep slumber must be the key to her longevity. She lay stretched out so quietly and thinly that her long body suggested not much more than a six-foot paper cut-out lying beneath a comforter. Konig sat down beside her, sipped his beer for a few minutes, but did not feel refreshed enough to go back downstairs to be alone and to work. Her breathing was so exceptionally quiet that tonight he inclined his head toward her and listened until he confirmed a regular little wheezy rhythm. Konig carefully lifted up the papers and magazines Emma had let fall from her hand as she had dropped off to sleep. "Iran and North Korea Sign Nuke Deal." "Number of Uninsured Americans Exceeds 75 million." "U.S. Combat Fatalities in Iraq hit 5,000."

The headlines captured the dizzyingly troubled state of the world made truly terrifying by the feeling, completely widespread, he was convinced, that our country is a vehicle without brakes or competent driver heading for the cliff's edge. Over all this what might a presidential per diem temporary ghostwriter do or accomplish? Or a language poet? Or even a lame duck president who had unleashed so much of it and now wanted to write a book! Konig emitted a sigh quite as dark as an oil slick.

"Jesus Christ, boy," Emma's voice startled him. "I don't appreciate the death watch, especially if it wakes me up."

"I'm very sorry."

"When I'm dead, I'll tell you. What are you doing here? White House closed?"

"Emma, please."

"Try fooling your auntie! What time is it?"

"Time for me to let you get back to sleep." He rose from the chair. "I'm really sorry."

"Oh stop with all the apologizing. You stay right here. Your wife called."

"What's up? What's the problem? Is she okay?"

"Is she okay? She's the pin-up girl of the plutocrats, isn't she? You've got to get up awfully early to pull the wool over these eyes."

Konig tried to play dumb, which actually came quite naturally to him these days. "And?"

"She said, 'Emma, I love you and I know you'll understand. Tell A.B. I'm going into seclusion and won't be in touch for a while, maybe a few weeks, but that great things are happening to me here.' Like what? I asked. Then she said she was such a hit reading that doggerel of hers to Tonoco Oil or whatever bloodsucking company they brought her up there for, that they've created a position for her."

"A position?"

"Bell introduced her to the Tonoco people. Apparently they instantly fell in love with your wife's poetry. Sit down, sonny. She said to tell you that she, little Anna Konig, is now America's first petroleum poet. They need their own laureate, their petroleum poet to be the spokesperson, through poetry, for their product."

"Oh boy."

"What have you done here, A.B.?"

"Boy oh boy."

"So I said to her, Honey, that stuff pollutes the world, kills the workers who get too close to it, and is a reason for 95% of the wars and the killing. You're going to write poetry about that?

"She said I should watch my blood pressure and let the verse she produced speak for itself. Fighting words, A.B. Oh, and then she said she was going into seclusion to research connections between poetry and fossil fuels through the ages. You getting all this? Quite a wife you have. It was important work, she said. We shouldn't begrudge her and that I should tell you."

"How can I reach her?"

"Seclusion, remember?

"I'll track her down through them. Through Cheever and Bell."

"You could." Then Emma paused, uncharacteristically. "Want some advice?"

"Not today, but thanks anyway. How do I reach her?"

"Don't do a thing is my advice. Not now. Not while you're tired. That's what my friend Jack London wrote in *New Masses*. You remember Jack? He was a wild one."

"Auntie, I never met Jack London, and neither did you." Konig paused. "And what did Jack have to say?"

"He said, Never make any serious life decision without a good night's sleep beforehand. Fatigue makes everything look worse than it is."

"What could be worse than this?"

"I'll tell you what galls me, A.B. You lied to me. She wasn't up there shopping, was she, you dissembling ungrateful boy."

"I didn't want to upset you."

"So you've done it double now. She's become a terribly misled girl. She's lost her way. While I'm working so they don't get you, they got her. The warmongers are coming after the whole family. What are you going to do about it?"

"Oh, Emma, she's just tired of being poor and unknown. What's the harm there?"

"A.B.," she said, sitting up in bed, as if sprung. "Deny that they've gotten to you too! Go on!

"What's to deny? How do you think Anna has become petroleum's poet laureate? So now you know. I just wanted to see what it felt like, finally, to have a little money too. To be...sought after."

"I'll show you 'sought after,'" and she lunged at him, lamely, with her pillow, "you pusillanimous rodent of a former radical, your parents are turning left, left, left in their graves, sonny. Honestly, A.B., what have you done?"

"Oh relax, it's just a temporary, trial basis that I said I'd do something. But my stuff, I assure you, is not very good. It's not happening for me. I'm

sure they'll see the mistake and fire me. It'll all be over soon, and it'll back to
seeing the world for what it really is, to being virtuous, and poor."

"Let's hope so."

"The one little problem I didn't foresee is how much Anna is hooked. If
they let me go, her pantoum career on the fossil fuels circuit will be over instantly, and guess who she'll blame? She'll think I've torpedoed her. She will
say that I deliberately sabotaged this great opportunity for her; and maybe
she'll divorce me."

"So what?"

"You can't mean that. You love Anna."

"Just because she divorces you doesn't mean she can't continue to live
here and to take care of me every now and then when I get older."

"You're old already, Emma. Very old."

"I've got more energy and change-the-world zeal in my nostril than
you've shown in your whole life. Awake and sing, boy. You remember we
saw that Clifford Odets play back in the heart of that dark Depression time?
No jobs. People throwing themselves off roofs, women leaving their babies.
It was terrible back in '35."

"Emma, I wasn't born in 1935."

"Well, you should have been. Had you lived through the Depression you
would understand that marriage, children, all that has to take a back seat
sometimes to the larger demands of a just society. Your divorce will be a
small price to pay for removing this blockhead of a president and his party
from office. A.B., stop pacing, and we'll think of something together."

Konig sat, and then stood, and then nervously sat down again on
Emma's bed, where his head dropped like a stone into his hands.

"The thing is, A.B., I see some genuine Fifth Column opportunities for
you here. Before they fire you, you need to write stuff that's so clever they'll
think it's good when it's actually bad. Awful. With people who believe their
own rhetoric as much as these people do, you'd be surprised how easy it can
be. Make 'em look like the fools they are. That way, you see, you can let
Anna have her little jaunt, and what you do at least will undermine them
from within. You'll be a spy, a Trojan horse of a ghostwriter for President
Brewster George, who deserves no less. And I'd be proud as hell of you, A.B.,
if you could carry that off."

"That's a tall order."

"Come on, nephew. Those people have huge blind spots, like I said. If they didn't, what could have possessed them to hire you? You just have to find more weaknesses like that and exploit them. How about it, A.B.? Activate those brains you inherited from me. Did you start already? Did you write anything?"

"I did. It's really awful."

"Excellent," Emma said. "Let me see it."

Sixteen

"Mr. Cheever," Konig said the next morning, when he sensed at least one of the lawyers had returned and he had three-stepped it upstairs. "How come you suddenly don't take my calls? Now I insist: Take me to my wife."

"Calm down, Mr. Konig. She's in seclusion, a writer's colony situation. You're familiar with that, are you not? You want to barge in and disrupt that concentration?"

"Yes, I do."

"Would you appreciate her doing the very same to you?"

"Mr. Cheever, I'm not negotiating visiting rights to my wife."

"Really? I thought that's exactly what we were doing. Have you...er...done your assignment?"

Konig, in point of fact, had worked with Emma and just this morning, before riding into the office, had raised a tremulous finger over the keyboard and emailed Kove the first significant batch of material.

"I kept my word. Now you keep yours."

"To the best of my understanding there is no binding arrangement regarding your wife."

"What is the problem here? Why are you keeping her from me?"

"If you visit, how will you prepare your next assignment for the President? And the next, and the next? Especially, given, you know, what happens between married people. I couldn't speak to this from personal experience although I see what I see. If you have a falling out, a fight, your work will be badly affected. How can it not be?"

"Cheever, just tell me: is she still at the Waldorf? It's a simple question."

"What makes you think your wife wants you to visit, wherever she is?"

"I don't care if she wants me to visit. I'm visiting."

"Quid est demonstrandum, sir."

"I will go downstairs in precisely two minutes, raise to my mouth my newly-repaired telephone, and call the White House."

Cheever went to the nearby desk, sat, and withdrew an elegant black pen and a small vest-pocket size folder from his jacket." Can we compromise? You speak to her, and then you decide if it's wise at this time to take the next step, actually to make a visit."

Konig pondered for a moment, then extended his hand, into which palm Cheever stuck a yellow post-it.

The following day, as a spray of light fell through the windows of the hotel's elegant executive suite, Anna Konig arranged herself into the lotus position on her writing rug. She was wrapped tightly not in the white silk robe that Konig had bought for her during the first week of their marriage and in which she often wrote early in the morning, but in a thick terrycloth—courtesy of the hotel; above it, another equally sumptuous towel turbaned her head. A blue writing notebook sat beside her on the floor like a magic lantern she was being careful to approach.

Thoughts of oil weren't coming to her naturally this morning. However, by summoning up the many words that rhymed with "butane" and "methane," associations were now just beginning to loosen; Anna breathed deeply, and began to compose.

Which was precisely when Konig barged into the room, with a flustered, red-faced Bell, his arms flailing, following in ineffectual pursuit.

"He threatened me," Bell panted. "Your husband threatened me if I didn't open up. So sorry, madame, to disturb your inspiration." He took out a handkerchief and mopped at his balding forehead. "If this is a measure of the violence you live with, Mrs. Konig, I would advise you to take legal steps immediately. I will be pleased to help."

Anna held herself very still on her tasseled writing rug. She seemed to be willing herself not to look at him.

"I pulled his tie," Konig said to Anna. "I did not threaten or assault him. We have to talk. Anna?"

Still she did not answer. She did not respond, she did not look his way.

"Legally, Mr. Konig, you have committed an assault."

"I'm thinking seriously about committing a real one on you right now! Take a hike."

"Dear Mr. Konig," Bell said, as a spirit of diplomacy returned, along with his breath, "We are allies in this great project, are we not? Are we not on a great poetico-political journey together?"

"A great what? Just go away," Konig said, pressing the diminutive lawyer steadily toward the door. "Be gone, on your journey, and be good enough to leave my wife and me alone."

"Breaking and entering," Bell cried. "Assault. Illegal trespass, violation of—"

"I'll show you violations." Then Konig drove Bell out into the hall and pushed him down on the chair outside door, where he had been keeping a sleepy guard. His mushiness to the touch was such that Konig felt as if were putting a large insufficiently boiled egg into its cup.

He returned to Anna and stood quietly before her. He sensed, rightly, that she was trying to will him back out that door along with the lawyer. "I took the shuttle. Anna?"

"You don't have to respond," Bell said, barging back in. "Our job is to monitor working conditions for the both of you and we will not be put off. Please leave Mrs. Konig to her work, Mr. Konig. Now."

"Excuse us for a moment," Konig said to her. Then he seized the lawyer by his lapels and raised him onto his toes. "Don't they teach you the meaning of a closed door in law school?" He dragged Bell, like a sack of laundry, with small loafers moving beneath it, out into the hall and down it until they arrived at the elevator. When its doors opened, Konig deposited Bell, pressed "L," and then returned to his wife.

She had risen, and the rug was folded and hidden beneath the bed. She now faced him with a lit cigarette dangling from her lips.

"When did you take up that nasty habit again?" She blew smoke toward him.

"I'm sorry you did this, A.B. Mr. Millard isn't going to like it."

"I *missed* you. I had to see you. Who's Mr. Millard?"

"Lawson Millard, the head of Tonoco. Where do you think Bell is off to? I don't have to put up with you, A.B. I'm a somebody now."

"To me you've always been a somebody. More than a somebody. My wife."

"That's just it. That's the rub."

"You don't understand. You're willfully blinding yourself to what's going on here, to the truth."

"Truth. Truth. You say those words as if you own them. You and Emma."

"Here's one truth I do know: The White House is after me, I'm reluctant to sign on with them, and you suddenly are anointed the whatever it is...."

"The Petroleum Poet, thank you very much."

"Come home, Olive Oil! This is laughable."

"You can be very cruel and selfish, A.B. Then you apologize and call it love. There's something wrong with this picture."

"There *is* something wrong with this picture. In plain language, they're using you."

"Really? To repeat to him whose ears are blocked up, it's just possible *The Journal* loves me on the merits. Can't I be the cause of my own success? I've got something now, A.B."

"Petroleum poetry?"

"Oh, wake up! I've taken an opportunity and made it my own. You take the conventions and transform them. Look what other people have done." She blew a big ring at him, like an undulating smoky life preserver floating his way; he half wanted to grab at it, but he stood still, and it settled on one shoulder and disappeared. "Feldman's become the homosexuals' oracle. Butler has been cashing in on Krishna and orientalism for a decade, and Lydia Bates's career has been sustained, I mean, is littered with discarded bras, confessional mood pieces, and just last year, that only book-length poem, a novel in verse, practically: 'an epic odyssey'—you remember the turgid flap copy, A.B., that drove you nuts?—'through the Scylla and Charybdis of child-bearing, divorce, and out into the scary open sea of independence.'"

"I know, I know," he muttered.

"You just don't trust me, A.B."

"Of course I do."

"Then why don't you see how I'm thinking way beyond the little niche of oil where, yes, a writer could easily get stuck, but not me. Not this writer. I am thinking large numbers of people that no poet has addressed in years, decades, centuries, millennia, if ever. "

"Millennia? Of what?"

"Of fuels, silly. Look, when you establish yourself, as I am doing, you have to be careful to have a poetic theme that will have reach into the past and into the future as well. Otherwise, you could set yourself up on a basis too narrow to support a career. You remember that guy Alan Lydel, how he made that huge mistake when he got hospitalized: he wrote a long series of poems on his victory over the cancer that had attacked his left testicle. Okay, it was daring, a big deal, and I give him credit for it, but a flash in the pan. Why? Because where could Lydel go from there? To his right testicle, maybe. And then what?"

"You're serious, aren't you? "

"A.B., with war in Iraq without end in sight, with the Iranians threatening the whole supply line, with central Asia up for grabs for pipelines, with the price at the pump periodically going stratospheric, I mean just because I start with oil, I don't have to stop. I can soon get them to think hybrid, solar, and wind. It's about energy, A.B. Sun, wind, sea. I mean poetry and petroleum are cousins as far as the eye can see. Oh…we're rhyming already."

"Won't you come home with me?"

"I need this."

"Yes, but I need this," he replied as he leaned toward her and Anna allowed him to kiss her on the neck. "And this. And this." He kissed her again, but her neck tasted odd, and he was very upset and tried not to show it. "And this," he said as he kissed her lips. But then she unpuckered, quite quickly, and walked ruminatively to the window overlooking the city.

"A.B., do you know what's going on out there? There are all these specialized fields fully or partially developed in the petroleum industry. Lawson explained it, and I tell you, it's mind-boggling. There's petro-accountancy and petro-economics and petro-engineering, and petro-everything. But there is still not a soul, not a division, not a company that takes poetry and literature seriously as an aspect of the fascinating world of oil. So when he told me this, guess what I said to him, A.B.?"

Konig entertained the idea that she had been drugged, or hypnotized. It wasn't beyond them. "Okay. What did you say to him?"

"This happened after I read 'Yelp' and then some of the new stuff for the first time."

"What did you say?"

"He congratulated me, and I said 'I will write the verses that will, from your industry, remove all the curses.'"

"Jesus," Konig muttered. Fortunately Anna had not heard him.

"And then he said right back to me, rhyming, 'Such sentiments are like money in our purses.'"

"I think I miss your old style, Anna."

"You're just saying that, and you're a very bad liar."

"'Ting, ping, pow, the blade strikes blue.' Remember that? I do."

"Liar."

"At least you were honest with yourself back then."

"If I'm doing what I want to do, that's honesty enough."

Konig saw one of Anna's spiral writing pads peeking out from under the newspapers on the table. He lunged for it and opening it up to the first page, he fought her attempts to grab it back, long enough to read, on the first page, in large printed block letters:

Hail, Shale
These are the words of Anna Marvell
The Petroleum Poet
Who lived on the Island of Manhattan
In the first decade of the 21st Century
Come, heed, listen

"Give that back, you creep. You have no right." She struggled harder to retrieve it, but Konig fended her off and skipped about the room flipping through the pages. Although he couldn't focus on the jottings and parry her at the same time, he had seen enough, and relinquished it.

"Creep!"

"Who the hell is Anna Marvell?"

"It's my pseudonym, Mr. Ghostwriter. My work will echo Andrew Marvell, who was not a slouch of a poet, you may remember, and also lived in an age of exploration and innovation. And as far as the style goes—because I know what you're thinking—the style is Biblical. The clauses don't exactly repeat, but they are haunting in a kind of parallelistic way. It's the style of the Middle East, A.B. It's the style of Sumeria and Iraq and Iran; it's the style of the Tigris and the Euphrates. It's where the oil is!"

"Let me see that again," he said and lunged for the notebook, snagging it back this time. In defending herself, Anna's robe opened. "Honey," he implored, "I'm your husband. I love you. You don't have to do this to yourself. We've worked something out. Emma and I."

"Give me that, A.B.," she said as she tied up. "You're just jealous because you've lost the flame, because you're reduced to ghosting. You just can't stand it, can you?"

"You might call yourself the Petroleum Poet, but if you keep writing this stuff, as far as I'm concerned you'll make yourself more the Bard of Lard."

"Then just scram out of here, A.B. You're getting in my way."

"I'm not getting in your way, I'm making your way. And you know exactly what I mean. Otherwise, who's going to publish this ..."

"That's what you think. Maybe you started it, but now I'm on my own. I'm launched. And if you think you can stop me, it's hubris time for you."

"I think you should tear that stuff up, come back home with me, I'll tell the White House where to get off, and life will return to normal."

"To waitressing and giving Emma massages? I don't think so!"

"Come on, Anna."

"Give me that notebook back."

"Petroleum Poet," he muttered as he read and walked around the room, and she followed grabbing at him.

At that instant, there was a loud rap on the door. Anna cinched up her robe tightly and sprinted toward it. There stood three men: a rebuttoned and restored Bell; beside him a heavy fellow in a dark brown suit whose darting eyes bespoke ex-cop or hotel detective. But the most incongruous of them was the thin, handsome man with a movie star tan, and very executively suited, who stood, leaning slightly against the door jamb, with open arms. Konig watched, in horror, as his wife fell into them. "Oh, Lawson," she said, "Lawson darling, thank god you arrived in time."

"Who is that?" Lawson Millard said.

"'Darling'?" Konig quite literally could not believe his ears. *Darling*, a word, a sound as in Anna's poetry, that in her former verse style, seemed, to arise from that man's mouth detached from all sense? For if that man was her darling, then who was he?

Konig dropped Anna's notebook to the floor and then he lowered his head, and charged the "darling," punching him in the ribs with all his might.

Seventeen

Early the next morning, in jeans and blazer, with an unshaven, poorly slept face that featured one full black eye and the makings of another, Konig stormed the White House.

"I will be with you in ten seconds," Raymond Kove said to him.

"Ten seconds and counting." Konig raised the arm bearing his wristwatch into a horizontal across his chest. The presidential advisor appeared to be making some adjustments to the small American flags on the color-coded 2008 electoral map before him.

"Mr. Kove," Konig said, "Your time is up. I want the government of the United States to give me back my wife."

"You really think the government just goes around abducting people?"

"As a matter of fact I do. Who is Lawson Millard?"

"Rings a bell. By the way, that's quite a shiner you have."

"I slugged your Mr. Millard, but then he caught me with his elbow. He got the worst of it, I'm proud to say. There's some left. You want a piece of it, fatso?"

"Get a grip. And, if I were you, I'd cut down on the boxing movie metaphors."

"Your goons threw me out, and it was very embarrassing and unceremonious. Now call them off. Call it all off. Send Millard back to central casting. Order Bell to put Anna on an airplane and send her home, to me."

"You're obviously very stressed, Mr. Konig. My advice is for you to lie down on that couch over there and gather yourself before you meet with the President."

"I signed a contract. I gave you what you want. I did not give you my wife. She is not part of the equation. Enough's enough."

Kove's eyes scrutinized him for a long interval, and then he spoke with measured gravity. "Neither the government of the United States nor the President's Legacy Committee has a policy to abduct, brainwash, or keep under detention the spouses of our per diem temporary ghostwriting consultant or any other subcontractor. If such conspiracy thinking persists, consider that it might be a holdover from your drug-taking past."

"My what?"

"We have files, Konig. Yours is phone book size and also makes for entertaining reading. Illegal trespass of a college building. Growing marijuana in one's bathroom tub. Trying to fob it off as an experiment in hydroponics for a chemistry course that you were failing. Really! Threatening an arresting officer. Illegal trespass again, most recently, March 2003."

"Yes, and proud of it. Trying to stop your private little war."

"One night in jail," Kove went on, unruffled. "Demanding vegan food—that's a new one, even for you. Vegan? Just to cause the system a little more trouble, eh, Mr. Konig? Let me see. There's also cursing the magistrate."

"All charges dropped. My record is clean as the driven snow, which is to say a lot cleaner than yours."

Kove turned his broad back on the ghostwriter and re-pinned several flags onto the map. "Mr. Konig, if you've got some trouble in your marriage, why blame this office and the President of the United States? And, more to the point, I'd advise you not to let such problems again interfere with the quality of your work. Take that testosterone and inject it into your prose, sir."

"How's that?"

"Before you meet the President, you and I need to go over...there are a considerable number of problems in the material you submitted."

"Oh?"

"Have a seat, and please get out your copy of the first chapter and other materials submitted."

"I didn't bring them."

"You came to make demands but not prepared to work? Mr. Konig, you are being well paid, and frankly these pages give me pause."

"I came to retrieve my wife, not to do copyediting."

"Here. I had a duplicate made for you, just in case. It's getting late. We can't go over all my…objections, but let's review a representative few before you go in there.

"Let's begin with the beginning, Mr. Konig; *Which way was east? The courageous cowboy had lost his way*…and so forth. Do you honestly think that's a smart way to start? Do you want our readers to suspect the hero's sidekick can't tell east from west? It doesn't exactly inspire confidence. What we need is a brilliant Muslim sidekick worthy of our hero, not a bumbling Muslim version of Walter Brennan. Really, Konig. I mean in your outline for chapter two do you have plans for him to be confused between north and south? Isn't it risky for the Muslim cowboy—the sidekick to the hero—to appear to be, geographically, anyway, a complete dummy, and for this to occur on line one of the proposed chapter one? Or don't you believe the opening of a story is critical, and should be perfect, down to the choice of every word, comma, pause, nuance, and so on and so forth?"

"Are you done?"

"Actually I've only just started."

"He's riding hell for leather, he's alone, among the cactuses, a tough, primal guy," Konig responded. "There are many other details that add up to a heroic picture. You're hung up on this one thing, which, by the way, establishes his religiosity, which is pretty important. Actually, I thought I had found a balance."

"Well, consider my response."

"Sure, considering is easy."

"All right, Mr. Konig, let's go to the end of this opening section where after he prostrates himself and proclaims Allah's greatness, and then that horse of his gives his 'little reins a shake.' You've got to strike that."

"It's a nice detail, it appeals to the senses, and it brings the reader in. Makes him empathetic."

"Mr. Konig, I'm not encouraged by your responses."

"What's the problem there?"

"The problem is that it's a flagrant rip-off of Robert Frost's 'Stopping by the Woods on a Snowy Evening' or some such."

"Echo, not rip-off. And what's wrong with that? Everyone who has gone to junior high in America has read and will recognize that poem. Readers will be flattered in a way they don't quite comprehend. The story will seem familiar in a manner that's unfamiliar, and in so doing will touch on the mysterious nature of—"

"—of what, Mr. Konig?"

"Of…what about my wife?"

"Mr. Konig, this is no way to deal with your anxieties about your partner. You must keep that separate from your work. You have another partner to consider, one who is equally worthy of your apparently scant attentions: namely, the President of the United States! This is your work now, and your worry, sir. Work well, be attentive to your clients, and, may I remind you that we are your clients. We are Republicans, and Robert Frost read at JFK's inauguration and we do not want even a distant echo of that. Legacy, man, legacy!"

"But you've challenged me to remind readers of the President's, uh, achievements; to shore up his image and also maybe help with voters in key states. New Hampshire is where it all gets started? Right after Iowa. So here, within a page or two, we've got him on a butte in New Mexico, where, symbolically, he bestrides that place with all the Hispanics, which you really need for legacy and election because we also see he knows a little Spanish already; and then, practically in the same narrative breath, we have this Frostian echo of New Hampshire. I haven't figured out Iowa yet, but here we are practically spanning the country in less than two hundred and fifty words. I thought I was being clever, almost brilliant, legacy wise, and succinct as hell."

"You're pulling my leg."

"I wouldn't go near your leg. Furthermore, I'd like to return to the subject of my wife."

"I'm less than happy with what you've produced, and yet it's already time to go to the President."

"What about Anna?"

"You just do your job. You turn in the chapters on time, and you make them hard-hitting, fast-moving, and legacy-laden, and you will have nothing to worry about. That's all I can tell you."

"You're so cagey."

"Are you prepared so that you don't waste the President's time? He's got Mars at nine thirty, Konig, and you have fifteen minutes."

"To do what? I just came here for my wife."

"You're on our time, friend. We set the agenda, and the President wants to talk to you about some of this...material. The Muslim cowboy's horse, for example, let me see, you call it an Appaloosa; I hope you will be prepared to talk about Appaloosas to the President; and also how the Muslim cowboy is going to meet up with the heroic character built on the President. He's not in the story yet."

"We're building up to him. Preparing the reader." Konig pulled himself up to his full height. "I will be making the Muslim posse members memorable, strong, brave, cactus-eating guys, former soldiers who fought in the Indian wars who also discover there's some Sunni and Shia in their background. They're on a common mission but don't know it quite yet and don't fully trust each other until...they ally themselves with a great Christian Texas-leader-type cowboy, whom they'll need for the leadership and vision thing, and who pulls it altogether. He is reflected in their rugged glory, and their fine qualities are in turn burnished by his purity and take-no-prisoners business sense. I see it as something like a religion-oriented, western-style *Dirty Dozen*, with the President a kind of Lee Marvin character who always has a copy of the Good Book in his saddle bags, but doesn't flaunt it and encourages recitations from the Koran as well as the poetry of Rumi and other Middle Eastern, peace-loving mystics around the campfire. You'll see. It's coming along just fine. I can tell."

"You can?"

"Of course, Kove. I'm a pro."

"Well, the next material you turn in had better be a little more *professional*. More than these general and, frankly, unconvincing notions. Don't you think that would be reasonable, at this stage?"

"Sure," said Konig, pleased with the barrage Emma had helped him to mount.

"I think he's going to want to discuss his character, along with the horse talk."

"Heroes, horses," Konig whispered to himself as his sweat glands began to process overtime. "No problem."

The President's scheduler came in then and announced that the Chief was ready. "For god's sake, here: at least walk in there with a pen or pencil. And, finally, do not discuss your wife with the President. That particular buck stops on my desk. Understood?"

"Just tell me," Konig asked, on the threshold. "What did the President think about the pages I submitted? Honestly."

"That's the damndest thing of all, Konig. He thought what you sent in was terrific."

Eighteen

When he entered, Konig was not sure what surprised him more: that the door to the Oval Office closed behind him for the first time without Raymond Kove also stepping in, or the astronaut, in full space suit, including boots, helmet, and dropped Mylar visor, who walked up to him and greeted him with a thickly gloved high-five.

The purple face-mask clicked up, and the face behind it said, "A.B., you got the right stuff, and so do I."

"Mr. President?"

"Whaddaya think?"

"Uh, dashing, sir."

Bending down on one knee before him, the President said, "Would you mind givin' the helmet a little twist, A.B.? I hate callin' in the Secret Service for everythin'."

"Very good, Mr. President."

"Well, every time I read your prose, A.B.," the President said, with his head finally liberated, "it just gets my own words flowin'. I really liked that Muslim cowboy and how religious he was and that thing he said while eatin' dust in the desert."

"Allah Akhbar."

"I mean for a cowboy to be speaking Arabic, if that isn't assimilation, the meltin' pot, the great American Dream, that you and I are livin' every day. I don't know what is."

Despite Konig's anger at how they had seduced and sequestered Anna from him and despite Emma's clever narrative strategy to embarrass the man, the President's approval and even delight in most nearly every word he had cooked up with Emma appeared genuine. That, combined with Brewster George's playful collaborations with him, were having a remarkable effect on Konig. The knot of anger and anxiety he had in his stomach, like a bad meal, was breaking up, and he commenced one of the best writing sessions he could remember in a long while. He felt suddenly and oddly no longer like the saboteur Emma had charged him to become but a real storyteller again. Notions and ideas—and fairly decent ones—began to flow.

"I really think, Mr. President, that we should play off the Texas heritage. I mean it's too good not to use to the fullest."

"I hear you, A.B.," the President said, leaning toward him, still in the space suit. "I'm with you. Go on."

"So whether we call the book, say, *From the Sands of San Antonio to Saudi*, or *From Texas to Tehran*, whatever it is, the hero has got to be from Texas and from god-fearing and oil-loving Texas."

"You're on a roll, and I'm rollin' with you."

"Therefore, I think your character, sir, should be called something like the Midland Kid. You are six feet two, tall at the shoulder, narrow at the hip. Handsome, of course, and there is a dashing scar on your—the character's—forehead."

"What's the scar from, A.B.?"

"It's just there. Scars are best when they are of mysterious origin."

"Natch. I get it."

"So you're out riding the range from having accomplished some mission, sir."

"What mission is that?"

"Like scars, the idea behind the mission should be left up in the air, at least for a while. Draws the reader in more."

"OK, A.B. I got ya."

"So you find this Muslim cowboy, and he is almost dead from thirst, and you give him water from your canteen."

"Who's he? What do we call the cowboy?"

"I'd say his name is Ibrahim."

"Oh, that's good."

"You got it, sir. And now we run with it. So Ibrahim is the first of the good Muslim boys that the Midland Kid befriends. The Kid is mysterious. He just does good things. Saves Ibrahim from dying of thirst, and when the water falls from the canteen onto his parched lips, it's like each drop is a blessing."

"Wow. Beautiful. Maybe the Kid can pick up a few more good ole Muslim boys, and, then, say, in another few days' ride, a farmer—"

"—Got it, Mr. President. Let's say a farmer, whose crops are mysteriously dying, and the Kid shows him where this foul run-off is coming onto the land, so that when the Kid fells a few trees, rolls a few rocks, he then dams it up, and, presto, the land flowers."

"Aren't we in the desert?"

"Good point, Mr. President. But this could be land on the fringe of the desert. And the farmer who is making the desert bloom is—"

"—A Jew!"

"Bingo. And now you've got the environmental and agricultural legacy bases covered too."

"And we need that real bad! I love collaboratin' with you, A.B."

"And what do you think of this, Mr. President? The farmer's name is Abraham. We work in the whole Judeo-Christian-Islamo thing right off the bat."

"So we got an Ibrahim and an Abraham and I—I mean the Midland Kid—is ridin' with them both. Fantastic. Where they ridin', A.B.?"

"Well, that's the part I'm working out for the next chapter."

"That's okay...say, what time is it?" the President asked. "It's hard to read my Rolex with this space suit on over it."

"My fifteen minutes are almost up."

"This is really good work, and the photographers are coming soon, A.B. Just tell me about the horse the Kid is ridin', and we'll call it a day."

"The horse?"

"The Kid must be ridin' a horse. I mean we haven't met him yet, but when he makes his appearance, his mount should be some really knock-out beautiful animal—no spots, no Appaloosas."

"Well, actually, Mr. President, I was thinking of a donkey."

"Come again, A.B.?"

"Well, I really wanted to distinguish your character. The reader is going to think horse, so why not upset a little expectation? That shows the author is on his toes, and through the author, that our hero is unique and really in charge."

"A donkey? No, A.B. I got to overrule you here in this line of thought. Politically, I couldn't hack that. Donkey, Democrat mule, ass. You hear where I'm coming from?

Konig swallowed hard but pushed on. "Right. I hear your concerns. On the other hand, don't you see, sir, that if you ride the donkey, you, the Midland Kid, are subliminally sending the message that you are bestride the Democrats. You are conveying the message through your transportation, so to speak, that the Grand Old Party is already the winner, and this takes you deep into launching your legacy, too, no matter if in addition to the House and the Senate, your party loses the Presidency as well. It's legacy insurance brought to you by fiction. Just what you ordered."

"Do me a favor, A.B., and don't talk to me about losin' again."

"OK, sir. The point, however, is that in the book we're operating in a realm way beyond November, and therefore, legacy-wise, we get the gang through Ohio and Florida and California and you're on that donkey. You win, legacy-wise, regardless of the facts on the ground, sir, as you often say."

"Konig, you are Klever, with a capital K. Let me think on that."

"And there's something else," Konig said as he stood and helped the President back on with his helmet to prepare for the next meeting.

"It's a little hard to hear, but go on. Raise the visor, please. Go on. Shoot."

"Who else do you associate with a donkey, Mr. President?"

"Huh?"

"Go way far back in time. Think Bible, Mr. President. Who rides a donkey into a town, and it's market day? And there are money-changers all over the place, and who turns over the tables, and—"

"Oh, Konig. Oh, A.B. Konig, for a little Jewish boy you are a devil. Jesus Christ!"

"Wouldn't the ultimate Christian cowboy be riding a donkey if he were in a western? Symbol, echo, the whole ball game?"

"That's powerful stuff, A.B. As I say, let me think on it. We've done helluva good work together."

"Thank you, Mr. President."

"Okay, go now because I know you want to begin workin' on the next chapter and the motivations, right? I mean once the posse's assembled, what are they going after? Right?"

"Right, sir."

"Very good," the President said as Konig went to the door, where the clatter of photographers was now audible.

After a nod of professional and manly understanding that hinted at a favorable start for the next working session, the President gave Konig another astronaut's high-five of farewell, and the ghostwriter went home.

Nineteen

"Oh, Auntie," said Konig days later as they were cleaning up from dinner and mechanically placing the Scrabble board on the cleared table, "have we got a problem."

"What is it now? You've been following the plan, haven't you?"

"Yes. And the words came—you saw. Paragraphs, chapters of them. And the President ate them up."

"Of course he loved them, the doofus. He'll be pilloried from Peoria to Pakistan when he publishes, and he may as well try to set up that presidential library of his in Haditha. So what's the problem, A.B.? I admit it's a little sad around here without that wife of yours, but please don't mope."

"That's not it."

"So?"

"What if, Emma, just what if...the book is successful?

"Impossible."

"But it's coming to me with such ease, we're having such a good time, Brewster and I."

"Did you just say 'Brewster and I'?"

"Yes, there's charm in that man, diamond-in-the-rough charm, a liar's charm, a narcissist's wink, and the candor of a man who won't sell you a bill of goods that he wouldn't buy himself. I hate to say it, but I kind of like him."

"He's a warmonger, A.B. He's a conservative with a selfish agenda, and a smile and quick compliment to plant it in your vulnerable little, anonymous ghostwriter's heart so you become an accessory to the crime. Will you remember that?"

"Sure, but—"

"But nothing. If you tell me any more about his charm, you can just go wash your mouth out. Bathroom's free."

"All I'm saying is what if, just what if some of the...the ease with which it's coming is getting through in the text? The underlying stuff we've come up with—the blatant way we're playing on ethnic and religious types—that's pretty low, I admit. Still, in parts, it's kind of funny."

"Don't you worry about that. You are playing a part is all, but it's like being an actor, while you're playing it, you've got to believe it. For example, I've been thinking about Saddam Hussein. We've definitely got to get some character like him into the book big time."

"So? I don't have a problem with that."

"Good, A.B. The problem is that yesterday he was a complete villain, but today because of that hanging he's a hero to half the world. A martyr, anyway."

"But he won't be that in our book."

"Don't you worry, sonny. In our book we're going to hang him good. Hang him the right way. Go on, A.B., write the scene. Get your hands a little dirty, A.B., morally speaking, and you'll accomplish some good. You've got to stick with it."

"We can't hang him yet, Emma. We need him for the story."

"Oh I'm in a hanging mood. Let's just write the scene. We'll use it later."

"Well, that's just the problem," Konig tried to explain to her. "Every step George takes in Iraq we might make fun of it if we can, along the way like you're doing, Emma, but we're still fixing him up, right? And if the book is a hit because people don't get what we're doing...I don't know. Maybe we're just outsmarting ourselves."

"Just relax and write what I tell you."

"You sure I'm not becoming a whore who discovers she likes the business."

"Piffle. What you are is a secret agent in the Oval Office. You're the Trojan Horse of ghostwriters. You'll see the city fall and you will have had a big part in it."

"I wish I could be as certain as you."

"Buck up, A.B. What's next?"

"Excuse me?"

"What's our next section? Aren't we supposed to work out the character of the bad guy, the enemy that the Kid and Ibrahim and Abraham are after? Or was it the Kid himself? Get me a Red Dog. This will be fun."

Konig now found himself staring at a white envelope, which he had not noticed before, protruding from Emma's cuff. "What do you have there?"

"Hanky."

"No, it's not."

"I was hoping not to have to show it to you, A.B. Yes, it's from her. Your beloved."

With unsteady hands, Konig removed the sheet of paper from the envelope Emma handed him. He sniffed in Anna's "turquoise of the night" perfume. He was stirred as he read aloud:

It may not be according to Hoyle
But drill we must to find that oil
So none in generations to come
Will be an oil or natural gas bum

Gone forever the crisis of seventy-three
Endless lines, prices climbing thru trees
For with bit and pipe and endless love
Find we now fossils below with God above

"Whew," said Emma. "Just when you think poetry can't get any worse, it actually does. My old friend Emma Lazarus would have a few things to say about that!"

"The worst part is," Konig said, "I think she's having an affair with one of the oil guys."

"How crude," Emma tittered.

"You were never married. You don't know. You were right that I should have turned the President down, and walked. Taken your advice that first day. Then this never would have happened."

"Well, why didn't you, you moral amoeba? Oh, don't answer. I know, I know. You ooze this way and that, corrupted by power, tempted by money, starved for a little attention—"

"But I'm broke, Emma. And I'm tired of taking money from my hundred-year-old aunt."

"A.B., I hate to see you wallowing so. I've got backbone for the two of us. You just keep me in Red Dog and play Scrabble with me to keep my neurons sharp, and I will do my duty, and yours too when necessary, you little hypocrite. Whatever happened to the moral high ground?"

"I guess I just fell off it," Konig mumbled as he paced the kitchen. "'Natural gas bum.' I might be a little more forgiving of her and her oily boyfriend if the poetry were better. 'OPEC OPEC, No more of your *dreck.*'"

"Yes, yes. Now pull yourself together, A.B. You keep losing sight of the opportunity this presents. The Midland Kid and the Petroleum Poet should not have you six ways to Sunday," she said. "Just play dirty by their rules, and prevail."

"I suppose."

"'I suppose. I suppose,'" Emma muttered as she slowly stood and, balancing herself at the edge of the kitchen table, folded up the Scrabble board, and then her copy of the newspaper. "A fella like you, when you start going around in circles, you should stop, and just go straight to the keyboard."

"You think she's really having an affair with—?"

"A.B., turn some of that misplaced jealousy and guilt into prose. I mean, what are emotions for? For example, just like we were saying a moment ago, why don't we just come out with it, the elephant in the room, and call our villain something like...what rhymes with Hussein? Wayne?

"That won't work."

"Duane?"

"Definitely not."

"Oh, let's not break our heads. Let's just call him Hussein. Brewstie will love it. He can be a Mexican varmint."

"I thought of that before, but an Iraqi in the Mexican territory a hundred years ago?"

"Okay. Make him *Don* Hussein."

"We better be careful we get this right, Emma."

"You worry too much. Okay now," she said rubbing her thin hands, as if she were sitting down to a fine meal. "Slaughters innocent peasants, rapes their daughters, emasculates the sons, strings up bodies from bridges. He even develops new techniques like blowing up whole stage coaches full of innocent women and babies with dynamite planted behind the roadside cactuses. Churches go up in smoke. The spires tumble. He plays all sides against each other, turns a range war into a kind of all-out war, town against town, farm against farm, within the territory, and he presides over it like an evil genius who drinks blood instead of water. What do you think of that? Whew! The clouds turn black, the sky is falling. Neighbors no longer trust each other. Havoc, bedlam, the whole dam ugly picture. You get it, A.B.?"

"Sure."

"And then something unexpected happens."

"I know. He escapes."

"You thought of that too? But didn't write it?

"No. Who escapes again. Sorry?"

"Is this the way you work with the President, A.B.? You're so distracted. I hope you muster more concentration, or you're going to raise some doubts. The way I see it he escapes from the little adobe spider hole or wherever they are keeping him, and he goes for his revenge like a hungry baby goes for the teat. A big piece of the Arab world was hoping this was going to happen anyway, so in this western it *does* happen. This time he has escaped hanging and he is really one pissed-off Arab, and he's threatening to be twice as terrible. Roadside devices blow stages to kingdom come. Trains are derailed, *senors* and *senoritas* are mangled. He's crazed, out of control. The sheriff and the local posse are unable to stop the guy. Yet he brings a kind of creativity and breadth to killing and mayhem never seen before in a western. How? Why? Because he just accepts that he is dead already. And since in real life he is really dead, Brewster will go for this big time. Guaranteed. Don Hussein is dead but is somehow still bestriding a world that is his to toy with as he wishes. Thanks to the hanging, readers will feel, some of them anyway, that his desire for revenge is now justified, so we can give him one helluva lot of gore."

"Okay, but we better be sure readers know that he's dead. That if he comes back, it's a little like an Iraqi Marley, a Muslim Christmas Carol."

"That's not bad, A.B. Right. Instead of a chain, Don Hussein can maybe walk around with a noose around his neck. Maybe we're getting ahead of ourselves like you say. Anyway, not to worry. This approach, you see, removes him from the normal human way of doing things. Nothing is beyond the monster. No horror too horrible not to engage in. Evil reigns once again throughout the territory; deputies are killed off like ants under his ugly boot, and no one steps forward to replace them. This makes a Clint Eastwood movie seem like a lullaby. You get it, A.B.? Whole sections of town are destroyed, and children play in the ruins. Ashes, ashes, all fall down! Boom! The fighting men are turning tail, the few *senoritas* left unviolated can't set foot outside; any girl walks outside, the hem of her petticoat is stained with the blood flowing in the streets. So they pull up their skirts, they make sure their mantillas and veils fit tight around their pretty dark eyes. People are beginning to say Don Hussein is not only devilish, but the very well-hoofed Vile One himself. The Devil Incarnate. Oh will Brewstie ever like that kind of antagonist. What a twist. Where's Clint? Bring it on, Eastwood. So, what's a body to do? Answer: The traumatized citizens send for their last hope and salvation, the Midland Kid. What do you think?"

"All right, I guess."

"You guess? I think we've been flaming brilliant. Things get so bad the Midland Kid absolutely has got to be found and his posse of Abrahams and Ibrahims come with their *jallabahs* and prayer scarves flying as they whip their sweating horses to the rescue in the nick. Damn, I'm good. A.B."

"Okay. So you do it."

That's when Emma whacked him on the head with her rolled-up *Nation.* "Listen, you, just how old do I have to become before I see my flesh and blood show a little spunk? Isn't a hundred years enough? Do I have to be two hundred years old?"

"Sorry, Emma."

She swiped at him again but missed. "Now you listen up: Thanks to your contract and the way that president likes every word you—we—write, you already have fangs in him." She whacked him again where his fangs should have been.

"I wish you would stop doing that, Emma."

"Well, just shape up then. I hate to see you this way, mooning over that girl who can take care of herself just fine. Do you know the only thing he can do, this Brewster, this worst president in American history? He is excellent at twisting you around his finger."

"How twisted?"

"Like a damn pretzel, that's how. Calling you the greatest thing since Owen Wister, Damon Runyon, and Louis Lamour. Really? They act nice, but they're not nice. They're very far from nice, A.B., those fear-mongering, oil-guzzling plutocrats. You say you see through their little show, but you are being played."

"No way."

"Then why won't you give it to them the way we've planned? That laptop they gave you? Crack it out. Work here with me, right in the kitchen. Think Upton Sinclair, think *New Masses*, think *Waiting for Lefty* and *Awake and Sing*. Show me how to use that newfangled typewriter, and I'll do it myself."

"Don't whack me again, Aunt Emma."

"All right, but you do understand that they now consider you their little liberal fool and left wing jester to manipulate as they please. That president is making you feel a somebody, but despite all the pretty words, you're nothing but a cog in the conservative juggernaut. I look at you and I hear the engines chugging."

"Maybe."

"A.B., you've got the chance to use him back."

"But he genuinely likes me."

"Oh boy. I don't think I appreciated how desperate you were. Perhaps I'm at fault for whacking you too much. That empties you of self-regard, I can see that now."

"I'm okay," Konig said, "but he does like me."

"Trust me. I'm your Great-Auntie. That counts more than being the commander in chief, doesn't it? You know how I hate getting sentimental, but I love you a lot more than they will, ever, but he is awfully smooth, the President. Still, who's *your* First Family?"

"You are, Emma."

"Damn tootin' we are. Small in number but a helluva spirit, and don't you forget it."

"Oh, I know."

"I guess I feel a little responsible too, A.B. the way I shoot you down all the time, like I said. You want to whack me back a little with *The Nation*? Go on. I won't break, it's always real thin, it won't hurt, and I finished the issue already. Go on. Whack away. I deserve it."

"That's all right, Emma. But thanks for the offer."

"All Mr. and Mrs. President had to do was smile at you, my poor boy, and you were a goner."

Having tangled enough with her, Konig walked Emma into the parlor, where the laptop that Cheever and Bell had presented to him sat, lid invitingly at a forty-five degree angle. He booted up, and when the screen lit, and the bells sounded, Emma said, "Now you're talking. What are you typing in there?"

"Just what you told me, Emma. Don Hussein escapes to strike again. Every ranch the Kid kicks the varmints out of, they come back when the Kid and his guys are down by the river praying or reading from their Bibles. What's the solution? The Kid obviously has to increase the manpower of his posse. That raises a problem: There's a finite number of good cowboys in the Territory. So the Kid begins to accept some of Don Hussein's deserters into the posse without doing much of a background check owing to lack of pencils, books, and so forth. And, just as you might think, pretty soon the Kid hears of depredations of mysterious origin. Some of these deserters are only alleged deserters. The Evil One is now, it becomes clear, infiltrating the Kid's own boys. The rock solid Solomons and Ibrahims and Abrahams are not so solid any more..."

"Pretty good, A.B., but too much on the intrigue. You need more blood."

"You do the blood, Emma."

"Oh it's easy, A.B. Some thing like...there's this new fangled invention, the telegraph. And Don Hussein now takes to sending a telegram to each of the victims he or his boys are about to waste."

"That sounds technological too, Emma."

"Maybe, but each of the telegrams arrives bordered in red. Upon examination, people realize it's not ink, but blood. Speaking of which," she said, "I was hoping you'd be able to slip in a request for my telegram, you know, between work sessions."

"Excuse me?"

"I was a hundred some time back, in case you didn't notice. And I never got the telegram the government is supposed to deliver to us centenarians. Will you bring it up with Brewster boy once he starts fawning over this text here? Okay? Once we get it in bad enough shape. I mean good."

Konig removed his fingers from the keyboard. "Let me understand, Emma. First you take me to the cleaners for being susceptible to presidential flattery, and now you actually care about some congratulatory telegram from him? You don't care that it might have a little blood on it too? Symbolically."

"That's right. I've got my weaknesses like anybody else. Anyway, I deserve it. So where is it, A.B.? It shows you what kind of government we have that they screw up sending out the telegrams on time, as if people who are a hundred and more have nothing else to do but sit around and wait for the mail lady. It's no wonder they screw up in Iraq. Goes to show."

"Goes to show what?" Konig said, but he wasn't really expecting an answer; consistency was not Emma's strong suit. Konig resumed typing. Practically acting out the scenes by his side, Emma was twisting and bending with all the mimed mayhem. It was quite a good aerobic workout for her, and Kong's fingers, flying across the keyboard, could barely keep up. There was something about her when she got to ranting about the government that just cleared Konig's brain and made his funk disappear.

"You're a bundle of contradictions, Emma, but you're also dynamite."

"That's right, and now, finally, just maybe, you know why, sonny. Because when a country's inherent contradictions come to a boil, that's the time to strike, or, in your case, write. Lance it, and comes the revolution. 2008 just might be the year."

"What revolution?"

"Oh, we'll talk about it later. Just keep typing."

That night as the Midland Kid rode up to El Poblito, strange noises filled the gunmetal gray sky. As he tied his stallion to the post and felt the handsome scar above his lip, the Kid listened intently to what seemed like the moaning of a wind that was lost and would never find its way home, or perhaps it was just the call of a lonesome and forlorn coyote. But it was none of those things, as he was soon to find out.

Don Hussein's twisted laugh was echoing down the length and breadth of the arroyo as the bodies of his victims tumbled down the banks. There were men, women, and young children, but it was the little babies the Kid fished out that troubled him most. Their dead eyes set in their heads like dark marbles had barely been given time by the fiend to register how wonderful the world might have been for them. The monster had snuffed them out so quickly.

That night, the rains, long overdue, also came. Yet they cleansed nothing, nothing at all. For they washed the remains of the campesinos into the tributaries that flowed to the surrounding pueblos. So that those who had survived him were now drinking water tainted by the dead bodies of their relatives, and they didn't even know it. The air smelled of flesh and of fear. People barricaded their doors, a paralysis set in that had been unknown in the territory even in the worst days of the raping and marauding conquistadores; even the horses refused to leave their barns.

"Oh, that's really bad."

"That's good."

"That's very bad. Over the top. Maybe take out the dead baby part. A touch too heartfelt."

"Okay."

"Very good."

Twenty

Whether working at home with Emma, or alone in the renovated basement, Konig had the uneasy feeling that he was now under a general surveillance. He was fairly sure the new phone was tapped, and every time it rang he visualized Bell, who had returned from New York, or Cheever, who had also returned from a mysterious fishing trip to some distant island (for he never recalled Cheever having gone fishing before), also flattening an ear against the basement door to eavesdrop on what they imagined were his top secret communications.

Most of Konig's calls, however, were only from newspapers trolling for him to subscribe, or from credit card consolidation services eager to help him reduce his debt. Normally, he might have been tempted to talk with one or two of these callers a day—he sympathized with their low-paying and often unrewarding jobs. However, since *The Midland Kid* project was launched, and the first few payments had been made by Kove, direct-deposited into his account, Konig, for the first time in years, had no time to chat, and was in fact on deadline every day, but he was not worried about money.

At least once a day the President of the United States himself also checked in with the ghostwriter. (To their endless frustration, Cheever and Bell never knew when.) Every time Brewster George came on, Konig was certain he was going to get the axe for having produced, thanks to Emma's subversive imagination, scenes that were outrageous, and even inflammatory, or worse. However, each Presidential conversation turned out exactly the opposite, as the most powerful man on earth had nothing but praise for Konig's prose. Thanks to Emma's uncanny touch, Konig was on a roll, and it just kept happening.

What's more, the President continued to be extraordinarily deferential. "Am I dialin' direct to you, A.B., as promised?"

"You are, sir."

"Brewster is your buddy, and he always keeps his promise."

"Thank you," Konig muttered, and, God help him, despite Emma's warnings that all this was just the orchestrated flimflamming of a manipulating politician, he felt as if he were talking with a true collaborator, an editor, a close reader, even a friend.

"I've been doin' some hard thinkin' about the Kid ridin' into town on the donkey, A.B.," said the President. "I know I said I was intrigued, but I'm wonderin' what you think about instead havin' our hero ride in on an elephant. I don't have to state the obvious, but Raymond and I feel that would consolidate and reassure the base. Do you think you can work that in?"

"Mr. President, how do I get an elephant into the New Mexico Territory?"

"I don't know, A.B. You're the writer."

"How about a camel?"

"We never thought of camels."

Well, Konig had. Arcane bits of knowledge that, over a career of ghost-ing bizarre subject matter, and which had seemed pointless after first use now deployed themselves in these conversations with the President with an ease that he found exhilarating. "I happen to know, sir, that early on in the twen-tieth century the U.S. Cavalry actually introduced camels into the south-west."

"No way, A.B.!"

Yes, sir, an experiment to see if they might be an alternative to horses. After all, there's a desert out there. I think it might have been General Douglas MacArthur's dad who got the idea. We'd have to play with the dates of our story a bit, but camels just might work."

"You don't say," said the President.

"On the other hand…" Konig ruminated, "I don't know if you want the Midland Kid astride a camel that people usually associate with the Middle East. That's the down side of the camels. You get my drift, Mr. President?"

"Indeed I do, A.B. And I appreciate the foreign policy savvy you are bringin' to this project."

"Thank you, sir."

"So I guess we're back to the elephant."

"There's always your traditional horse that the hero can ride, but would that be dramatic enough for you, sir? I mean for the Kid."

"Well, that's right, A.B. On the other hand, how am I gonna catch up to Don Hussein and the varmints if I'm ridin' some slowpoke pachyderm?"

"Good point, Mr. President. I would think that Raymond might have called that to your attention."

"Right you are, A.B. He should've checked out if maybe there's a breed of elephant there that can outrun a horse."

"We don't want to strain credulity, Mr. President."

"Don't you worry your creative head about that. I've got plenty of staff workin' on the credulity angle."

"What about a circus, Mr. President?"

"Go, A.B. I hear the cogs clickin'."

"Well, if there were a circus, a traveling circus passing through the Territory at the time of our story, then there just might be this escaped elephant. That's how we get Jumbo into the story."

"But wouldn't the Kid have to return the elephant sooner or later to the circus folks? Otherwise I leave the impression that I'm ridin' around on stolen property. And we are to give nothin', and I mean nothin' to these people accusin' our side of profiteerin'."

"Point taken, Mr. President. Maybe we should stick with a horse, a beautiful white one that looks like an American horse, a big stallion, say, but we have one of the characters comment, maybe Ibrahim does this, that the horse also has Arab bloodlines. That's good in a horse, Mr. President, and then you have the Arabs contributing to the American effort, mirroring the, you know, the political realm."

"Mmmm, a Muslim-American thoroughbred. Our Saudi good buddies will definitely appreciate that touch. Boy, A.B., are you ever a problem solver."

"Thank you, sir."

"Now, as I've said before, you can cut out the 'sir' business. We are friends collaboratin'."

"Thank you, sir. Mr. President."

"Call me Brewster."

"I can't do that."

"Brewster."

"I can't."

"Yes, you can."

"Brewster," said Konig. "I'm honored."

"Okay, A.B...am I taking up too much of your time?"

"My time? No, sir. Brewster."

"All right, so let's look at this cantina where I make my appearance in the story. I love the little Mexican place you made up, El Poblito, and the way you do the atmosphere—the dust and that sweet accordion and guitar music. Man, I can really visualize the place: the smoky senoritas, the rough bar, that board stretched across barrels of hardtack, with those beautiful bottles of tequila, ah yes, the beads hangin' from the doorways, and I can practically hear the music like in a Johnny Cash song. But—"

"—I know, sir."

"Brewster."

"Right."

"Well, I don't want to be encouragin' drinkin'—"

"—I hear you. How's about a vegetable bar, Mr. President? Juice."

"Juice from what, A.B.? It's the desert."

"Cactus juice? Tough juice for tough, hard people like the Kid."

"Lemme think on that, A.B. Cactus juice?"

"Prickly on the outside and sweet on the inside," said Konig as he fiddled with his pencil and peered into the corner of his basement for Norman to wave to, he was so relaxed. "It might remind readers of the Israelis, Mr. President, because that's sort of a symbol for them, for the *sabras*, the native-born Israelis, who present a prickly, no-nonsense, shoot-em-up exterior, but beneath the cactus thorns they are sweet and peace-loving as koalas, and, I might add, are also willing to negotiate if you give them half a chance. It might help you pick up some Jewish support for your legacy projects. Jews are big on legacy. And that cactus is an image that, pardon the pun, cuts a lot of ways."

"I wish Raymond were around to hear this. Our temporary per diem ghostwriter consultant is one helluva political strategist too."

"I'd only add that a cantina selling cactus and other healthy, natural juices and berry drinks also echoes our opening scene with all the Saguaro cactuses. A sense of place is important to the book. A sense of our vast America, the land and the deserts that are open, with all those cactus arms nearly waving, saying, 'Welcome, Bienvenidos,', so that a sense of hope is created that there's plenty of room still left out there in the desert for future housing for all the illegal immigrants, to build communities, one, two, three new Los Angeles-type cities among the cactuses, if they decide to get legal."

"I'll take all the help I can get in L.A. I'm absorbing it all in, A.B., and I am mighty happy."

"Thank you, Brewster." There was a telephonic silence now, one in which Konig heard odd noises and wondered indeed if the telephone line was being tampered with by Cheever and Bell, or if the NSA or CIA were listening in. On their very own leader and commander-in-chief? Yes, anything was possible, of course. "May I ask you something, Mr. President? It's a small matter, really...about a relative. You're not giving me too much time, Mr. President?"

"Brewster."

"Brewster, sir. You sure you don't have a security briefing to rush off to? Joint Chiefs? Lunch with, I don't know, the national security advisor? I know you're keeping an eye on, well, you know, lots of hot spots."

"Don't you worry, A.B. You are far too modest. Your happiness is key to the success of this here novel. Now just what can the Executive Branch do for your one-hundred-year old great-auntie?"

Twenty-one

Several hours later Raymond Kove, under full control, as always, yet quietly preoccupied, was in the Oval Office. While he listened, the President vigorously rearranged the several, red, blue, and yellow briefing books on his desk.

"But, Mr. President, there is absolutely no precedent for this. Since there is no record that Emma Konig is, or ever, was a citizen of the United States, how can we go sending coveted a letter of congratulations to her, or to just any centenarian who asks for it? Maybe she's not really one hundred. There's no birth certificate, which makes us think she's an illegal alien centenarian."

"Don't you think you're being a tad of a hard-ass on the old lady, R.K.? By the way, I had a terrific session with A.B the other day. We did a little jump roping between bouts of work; in addition to all that scribe's talent and political savvy, he's a pretty good athlete."

"A remarkable man," Kove said through clenched teeth. "Returning to this Emma woman, Mr. President, it is really a matter of national policy. If word gets out that Konig's auntie gets a letter, we'll be swamped by requests.

"Truth be told, Mr. President, it could get very political very fast. We need the vote of the extremely elderly if the party is to hold the presidency, as you well know. But I'd think really hard about offering this old Ukrainian socialist or whatever she really is a letter bearing the great seal of the United States."

"Socialist? But you told me she taught public high school in New York back in the Thirties."

"Yes, but they had no proper background checks then."

"Raymond, spit it out."

"Overall, Mr. President, I have been having some serious second thoughts in general about K…"

"…No, no, R.K.. Don't you go outsmartin' yourself. Besides, I got some bigger plans for the ghostwriter."

"You do?"

"Well, maybe a sequel to *The Midland Kid*. That's right. So what do you think?"

"My recommendation is that we should have a full-scale review of this material he's been providing before you involve him more in your legacy. This chapter, for example."

"No, no, Raymond, don't go there."

"It's not envy speaking, sir. Look at these pages, please, on their merits. I know you compliment him a great deal, and that is astute of you, Mr. President, because your enthusiasm and your constant praise are what he apparently requires. However, some of that enthusiasm is not quite deserved, sir, for surely, Mr. President –"

"—Surely what?" the President echoed impatiently.

"Surely the material, at minimum, needs major reworking."

"Oh, well, yeah. I guess. Here and there, sure. But I'm growin' irritable myself, R.K., every now and then as I look at these single digit approval numbers. Seems the ghostwriter's doin' a bit more for me than you are these days. So put those pages away, and let's stop finding fault. I know some of the material practically by heart, I admire it so. Let me see where you are…yup, right there he's got that whole posse comitatus assembled. A.B.'s got that cowboy from Minnesota, he's got us a blacksmith from Ohio, he's got that funny little fella who's a snake handler from Florida who, A.B. says, is going to deploy the snakes he uses in religious services—you see how smart our ghostwriter is, Raymond. He's going to use those snakes in a later scene when he will have the serpents of the Lord echo the rods that Aaron and Moses threw down in front of Pharaoh. A.B. is going to have the Florida fella toss the vipers right at Don Hussein just when his gang of varmints think they got the best of me, I mean, the Midland Kid. Raymond, have we got a movie here to make old Charlie Heston jealous or what!"

"Can we look at the text more carefully, Mr. President?"

"I thought I was pretty careful and detailed there. But if you mean the politics of it, like you counseled from the beginning, it's there too, isn't it? That posse has got a member from each and every one of our core states. A.B. is doing exactly what you told him to do. You should be proud. This is your baby too, Raymond."

"Mr. President, have you really and truly read every word?"

"Really and truly, Raymond. And then some."

"All right, will you permit me, Mr. President?"

"Sure, sure, Raymond, if you must. Go on."

"Well, in this scene, here where Don Hussein has you seemingly trapped, you and the cowboy from Minnesota are stuck under two railroad ties at the back there behind El Poblito—"

"Yup, that's a gem all right."

"And Konig has you and the Minnesota boy calling out. May I quote it, Mr. President?"

"Sure."

"'Akyaaa beyt tadkeetha,' he writes. Then he goes on, 'zaadeg lee d-asheeg eeday men perdey devshannay-y, dayenu.'"

"I do like that."

"Mr. President, do you recognize the language, sir?"

"No, but it sounds painful, the language of affliction and pain, A.B. says just what the scene calls for."

"Well, sir, I didn't know what language either. At first. But let's go on. Later, here, in the next section, when Minnesota Joe gets it, when Don Hussein drives one of those railroad pegs through his eye, the Minnesota character cries out again in pain, 'Een youdaya naa ella-bhaw yowman lama hweath ba-medeeta.'"

"Ouch," said the President. "Ooooie."

"Mr. President, when my suspicions were aroused, I got some of the boys at State and CIA to look at this text, and you know what we found? Konig has you and Minnesota Joe crying out in pain in Aramaic."

"No!"

"That's right, sir."

"What's it mean, Kove, the Aramaic?"

"Mr. President?"

"Yes, something unclear about my question?"

"Well, no sir. But actually…in point of fact…the fact that it's Aramaic, Mr. President, that's the point. Don't you think Konig is trying to put one over on us?"

"I asked what the words mean, R.K., and you are evadin' me."

"Sir, the boys ascertained it was definitely Aramaic, a Middle Eastern language of ancient origin, and it probably means…it probably means, my god, take that peg out of my darn eye!"

"Our boys still a little short on the old language skills, Raymond?"

"One of our Jewish agents thinks it might have something to do with the Passover Seder. But he's not very observant, so it's still a guess."

"My, that's very reassuring. A.B. probably knows exactly what it means."

"But, Mr. President, it's Aramaic! He has you speaking, whatever the words mean, precisely the language of Jesus."

"And why not? If Aramaic is good enough for Mel's whole movie, why not for a few lines in our book? Why not even consider that little donkey turn A.B. came up with? It's just fine marketing. A.B. shows another facet of himself through that scene, Raymond. And I thank you for helpin' clarify it."

"But, Mr. President, he's setting you up to be accused of blasphemy right here, is the way I read it."

"Nonsense."

"May I pursue this a bit further?"

"Sure, sure, I spose your mouth's got to get its exercise this way. Shoot."

"Assuming you can bask in the Jesus association safely," Kove said, "how did Konig explain precisely where Minnesota Joe and the Midland Kid learned their Aramaic, Mr. President?"

"Well, he's on the case, R.K. It was part of our last workin' session. Lemme see. There's this minor character, an itinerant peddler named Solomon sells pots and pans and trinkets and mantillas and such for the ladies around El Poblito. Stands for the small businessman/entrepreneur, America's prime creator of jobs, even back then. He comes out of Texas, and he also happens to be kinduv a rabbi, part time."

"Really. But Mr. President—"

"—The fella's a refugee from the Revolution of 1848 in Germany, A.B. says. I know you know about the Reagan Revolution, R.K., but how 'bout this one? You heard of it? Listen, we can't know everythin'. That's why we hire the ghostwriter! You see," said the President, "in Germany Solomon was this brilliant student of Near Eastern languages at the University of Heidelberg or some such, but then when the Jews got their butts kicked out of school there, Solomon looks west, hops a Yankee Clipper, and follows his dream—and a cousin—to the New Mexico territory, come by way of Corpus Christi. There Solomon tutors the cousin's kids while he does some business, and the gang, the posse learn a little Aramaic in their down time from trackin' Don Hussein when they go shoppin' at Solomon's wagon. When Solomon's cousin's kids are among victims of Don Hussein, he joins our posse. Whaddaya think?"

Raymond Kove's lower jaw drifted down from the upper.

"Maybe we oughtta get ourselves a few more Solomons over at Langley. Get ourselves a little real intelligence for a change?"

"Perhaps, sir."

"Don't you fret, Raymond. You help A.B. remain content and if that means gettin' his great-aunt her darn telegram, will you please see that it's done?"

"All right, sir," said Kove.

"And one more thing," said the President. "Maybe I'll put a little personal note on the telegram to the auntie, if you think that's a good idea."

"Oh, very good, Mr. President. Very good."

Twenty-two

"Norman, wasn't it great the way the President said he was personally going to get Emma her telegram?" The ghostwriter averted his eyes from his mesmerizing screen and scanned his office floor to judge where the rustle had come from. "We will not let her live this one down, will we, Norman?"

Konig dropped to the floor and, moving around on his knees, inserted his hand between two piles of stacked papers. He waited, hoping for a familiar mousey softness against his fingers, or for the tickle of a thin white whisker. "Norman, show yourself."

The only response, however, was a deep silence.

"Norman, why at this moment are the two creatures I feel closest to in the world the President of the United States, the most powerful, and you, among the weakest? And Anna, Anna. I feel a million miles away from my own wife. Norman, even though, to the best of my knowledge, you have no mouse partner, still may I discuss a marital matter with you?"

Konig sighed, got off all fours, and resumed his seat. He applied himself to fleshing out Don Hussein. He had to give the killer some back-story and a few more signature details. Not too much that might interrupt the flow, but enough color and of the kind to render Hussein a worthy opponent for the Midland Kid.

Konig perused the newspapers, and began jotting some paragraphs about a part of the territory he hadn't explored before. He toyed with the idea of giving the Kid a beautiful ranch called Zona Verde. It would be the only area still untouched by Don Hussein's predations. However, he immediately saw some downside: it might make the Kid appear too rich, and, even more serious, by this morning's accounts in the *Washington Post*, mortar rounds were now falling in Baghdad's Green Zone. Konig tore up the Zona Verde drafts, and returned to Don Hussein's physical qualities.

He considered making Hussein satanic, with horny devilish feet that the killer could barely stuff into his large boots, but Konig thought the better of it; it was preferable that the evil should be of human origin. He deleted pages and gave the killer normal feet, but ones that smelled in the night so that none of his *compadres* wanted to be near him as they lay in their colorful Indian bedrolls around the smoky campfire near the mouth of the cave. The cave was where they hung out and conspired when they weren't terrorizing towns or ripping the bodices off the milky white torsos of the *chiquitas* in the environs of El Poblito.

Don Hussein considered the deference of his gang a sign of respect. Such was his self-regard, he had no clue the men were ridiculing him—out of ear-shot—and telling each other that his foot odor, akin to a horrific allicinic mélange of garlic and bat guano, might just get them all killed because it would lead the law, namely, the Midland Kid, right to them. How do you tell the worst killer in the history of the Southwest that, even as a matter of strategy, he should bathe more often?

Ah, thought Konig: at a critical moment, when the Kid and Don Hussein are about to go after each other for the first time, Ibrahim, the Muslim cowboy, who is the Kid's right hand, dramatically walks between them, and wordlessly falls to one knee. Even while the hammers of the revolvers are cocked, Ibrahim holds out his hands, showing he would like to be of service to Don Hussein. While the two adversaries stare each other down with hate in their eyes, and the respective gang members are positioned behind the rocks and boulders above to spray the mesa with lead, Ibrahim carefully removes Hussein's boots, with their blindingly fascist shine, and pours water from his canteen over the killer's stinking feet. Such a gesture of hospitality, friendship, and with echoes of Abraham cleaning the feet of the angels in Genesis, will surely...

Konig paused in his typing both because what he had written was making him nauseous again, and also because he wanted to search the silence one more time for a clue to Norman's whereabouts; for the mouse had recently been alarmingly aloof. Konig held his breath, but the moment of complete silence yielded not a rustle, not a crinkle of paper, no telltale sign.

Taking a cue from the material he had just written, Konig went to the shelf near the window, the coolest place in the office, and retrieved from its baggie a small square of smelly, redolent camembert, which he kept for the special occasions, such as this one, when he absolutely required the companionship of the mouse.

Konig spooned an especially generous chunk of the delicacy onto a post-it and positioned it in the usual spot between computer mouse and keyboard. As the aroma filled up the basement, such that wildlife for miles around might this instant be on their way to the Cheever and Bell building, Konig waited expectantly. After fifteen minutes, when he realized that the lure was not working for the creature for whom it was intended, the ghostwriter ate the cheese himself and decided his day at the office had come to an end.

Konig filled his backpack with the heavily marked up pages about Don Hussein and decided to go home, where Emma would surely be able to improve on them. Once she had a Red Dog or two, her vitriol against Brewster George, who from the safety of his office had recently decided to send yet more brigades of young Americans to Iraq, would all rise again, her anti-government rant would begin—See how he's killing off the country's future teachers! The social workers, the doctors, the…—and Konig would have material aplenty for ten chapters.

Yet when he arrived home, the rooms were as absent of Emma as the office had been of Norman. Konig searched everywhere. She was so thin and flat you could sometimes even miss her in her own tightly made bed. Fearing the worst, Konig lifted up the yellow comforter, but found the bed empty and cold.

Suddenly remembering that the Ambassador—in lieu of considerable unpaid rent—was to have been keeping Emma company today at the zoo, Konig went back through the rooms on the parlor floor, then out and down the steps to Paramahansa's basement apartment. He now saw in the moonlight what he had missed coming in: taped to the metal panel of the mailboxes was a small envelope bearing his name in old fashioned script.

Opening it, Konig found on elaborately embossed stationery from the consulate of Brawada these words:

```
Revered Landlord: Have taken Great-aunt Emma to a
reception my country has arranged for non-aligned
members. Also, we are pleased to present you with our
consular rent herein. Respectfully,
             Paramahansa Yogan, consul, and neighbor
```

Konig checked his watch. Eight o'clock was normally Emma's bedtime, and it was now nearly eleven. Although he could not quite visualize his harridan of an aunt among polite, bowing, non-aligned diplomats sipping white wine, he certainly didn't begrudge Emma a little excitement. Yet how long could food and drink last at a reception at the embassy of the world's most impoverished atoll?

Konig decided to get into bed with an old-fashioned yellow pad and pencil and write some more on his own, or at least try to improve on the description of Don Hussein's intensely black and beady eyes until Emma returned.

In addition, he wondered, as he pocketed the Ambassador's check, climbed back, and went upstairs, what had happened to enrich Brawada so suddenly? How could they now afford a full year's rent and elaborate party?

He applied himself to arranging the bedding, including the pink-fringed oval pillow bearing the face of Emily Dickinson, which Anna always used to support her writing pad. Its presence, however, only distracted him and made him wonder where she was at this very moment. He imagined Anna and Lawson Millard sashaying like Ginger and Fred, and…No, Emma was right. He must give Anna the freedom she seemed now to require, and not violate it even in his possessive imagination. Instead, he must finish the writing job he had started.

So Konig made a comfortable support against the headboard, flung Emily Dickinson across the room, took a deep breath, and began.

Minnesota Joe had just come back from watering the Kid's horse, Duke. The Kid was looking into camels for all of them, but they had not been able to find a source, and Solomon was off by himself, risking capture by Don Hussein, to find where they might pick up some secondhand dromedaries for cheap. In the meantime, they continued to use horses, and the Kid's stallion, Duke, had been spooked by a basket of copperheads and rattlers they figured that Hussein had planted by the road near El Poblito. Joe had put Duke off by himself, away from the posse's other animals, to commune with Bucephalus and all the gods of the horses, or think on whatever horses thought about at night while tethered and earthbound, when, occasionally, like humans, they might cast their eyes up at the star-studded sky that now sparkled over the territory.

"Maybe that horse of yourn will calm the hell down," said Joe, "'fore he scares the piss out of half God's creatures."

"I sure hope so," said the Kid as he pondered flames of the campfire that were lighting up his handsome, slightly scarred visage. A ripple of goodness moved across the Kid's chiseled features, and he said, "I wish you would lay off the cussing, Joe."

"Sure, boss," said Joe.

"Shall I fall on my knees and pray for forgiveness with you?" asked another of the compadres.

"That won't be necessary tonight," the Kid said. "You're a good man and you've had a hard day. Let's rest, and when Duke shuts up his horsy face, we'll offer up our prayers from this Bible I always keep right here in my saddlebag. Then we'll hit the sack so we can rise before dawn and be well rested to kick Hussein's butt tomorrow. How's that for a plan?"

Just then Minnesota Joe, hungry as all get out, squatted down to a mess of pork and beans and was just beginning to mop it up with a slab of hardtack when along comes Ibrahim, the Muslim cowboy from along the Ohio (near Detroit), and with him comes Solomon too, bedraggled and upset that no dromedaries were available anywhere in New Mexico for love nor money so far as he was able to tell.

"Don't be discouraged," the Kid tells him.

"Thanks for the support," says Solomon.

Minnesota Joe offers Ibrahim and Solomon some of the pork and beans, which elicits the Kid's explaining that they should be sensitive to the eating requirements of the Muslim and Jewish posse members. Without missing a beat, Joe pulls out his Bowie knife and offers to spear the chunks of pork up and out of the pot that's simmering on the campfire. Ibrahim is grateful, but he explains that the mess of beans is still all porked up and tainted and doesn't meet the strict halal dietary standards he's trying to live by even on this lawless frontier...

At this moment the horses suddenly begin to make strange whinnying noises in the night. Joe, at first, thinks that Duke is just having a horse's bad dream, but we are not sure. For maybe something more sinister is afoot among the horses. Maybe Don Hussein is camouflaging his attack by approaching from among the horses as he prepares to strike.

Leaping up, the Midland Kid draws his long-barreled revolver and slowly lowers the hammer. He is just about ready to squeeze the trigger, when Abraham, the farmer turned gunfighter, emerges from among the swaying tails and sweaty haunches of horse flesh.

"Sorry, Kid," he says, "I was just answering nature's call and I took a shortcut back."

"Shortcut to the world to come," the Kid says, easing down the hammer of his Colt. "Each member of this posse is precious to me like a brother, and I almost killed you. Gimme a hug."

After the Kid and Solomon embrace, they all settle in around the campfire, as cans of beans, pouches of greasy hardtack, and a boiling pot of water with honey (because the Kid doesn't drink coffee—caffeine jitters up your aim) are passed all around. A heated discussion ensues about the next step: Whether the Kid should lead them in an attack on Don Hussein's nearby smoky cave right now—perhaps as soon as this very night—or whether they should delay.

Ibrahim is for waiting, in part because he's still hungry and feeling weak as the tasty pork and food odors are driving him crazy, and also because he spotted several of Don Hussein's henchmen in town today.

"They're like wasps," he advises the Kid. "Let's wait at least until sundown tomorrow, when they all have returned to the nest and we can get them in one attack. We can wipe them out, annihilate them from the face of the earth."

Red, the Florida cowboy who handles snakes and who hails from the swamps that would become Broward County, where he learned to understand and to tame serpents, agrees. Abraham and Solomon, however, both fear a fresh atrocity and think they shouldn't wait but strike right away. Solomon's cousin was recently killed by Don Hussein's men and the little man's lust to even the score is clear to all.

Minnesota Joe burps and says they should not let vengeance blind them as they make their move.

"The desire to avenge is beautiful," counters Ibrahim.

"Perhaps," retorts Joe, "but it can also be construed as weakness, my friend, and weakness as impotence."

"I like this Colt's hangin' from this belt 'round my waist," says Red, "and maybe I don't know much, but this I know: it ain't impotence."

In the meantime, Ibrahim is fading. The Kid sees this and suggests he tuck in. "We're not a debating society," he says. "Our actions will speak for us."

"Right, Kid," says Joe.

"I'll tell you this, though," the Kid says as he stands and stretches his tall body toward the firmament. "When we do strike, vengeance will have nothing to do with it, for justice will be our guide. People may call it vengeance and they may revile us—it's hard to know what history will say—but I ask you, what is vengeance but a kind of preemptive justice? Or for that matter, what is justice but pre-emptive vengeance, and that's more than that devil Hussein deserves."

"Amen, brother," says Abraham, and as he kneels to arrange his sleeping roll, he discovers a mess of porkless beans in his kit, which he'd forgotten about, because he too is trying to maintain the Jewish dietary laws, just as Ibrahim the Muslim is honorably trying to maintain his in the wilderness. As the Kid smiles above his guys, Abraham offers Ibrahim the beans, and Ibrahim gratefully slurps up the porkless legumes as the cowboys begin to doze and then snore. As the dying embers of the fire glow their last, the Kid says, "I'll take the first watch."

Twenty-three

"Whoa, this chapter really has gone downhill," the President was saying to Konig several days later as they jogged around the Rose Garden. "That campfire scene, whew…let me put it this way, A.B: I could smell the beans, and they were a mite stale, A.B. What happened?"

"I don't disagree with your judgment, Mr. President," Konig said, breathing hard to keep up with the Jogger-in-Chief. How could he reveal to him that Emma had not returned, and without Emma he had not been able to revise, to polish, and to achieve her satirical legerdemain?

"What you say, A.B.?"

"Maybe it does need another once over," the ghostwriter panted. "I'll get it right this afternoon, if I survive this run."

"Appreciate your honesty, A.B. I guess even the world's very best ghostwriter can hit a bad patch."

"Yes, sir, thank you."

Konig was doing his best to match the long stride of the President, who set a torrid pace. "Why, look, there's Raymond gettin' ready to join us for a few laps. Let's slow down to a turtle's crawl. He seems to want to talk with you about the chapter. You don't mind, A.B.?"

"Well, Mr. President…"

"Oh, I know you two have your little disagreements sometimes, but what the hey, we are in this together. Yo, Raymond!"

As the President accelerated past meticulously groomed hedges of box, and nearby gardeners whose Secret Service earpieces curled out from beneath their floppy, beige canvas caps, it escaped neither the advisor nor the ghostwriter that the President had purposefully left the two of them to jog alone together.

"Where's my great-aunt?" Konig said.

"I don't know what you're talking about," Kove panted.

"First my wife, and now Emma. Where have you taken them?"

"Really, Mr. Konig."

"Don't you 'really' me, you tub of lard. Ever since I signed the contract to work on this book, not a leaf drops by my window that you haven't blown it."

"How come that chapter you turned in is so god-awful, Mr. Konig? Tell me that."

"It's a little rough around the edges. It's not so bad."

"Konig, it reads like a pathetic pastiche of a Mel Brooks film. The President saw right through it. Do you think we hired you to portray him, the Midland Kid, slouching about the campfire, with people making fools of themselves, like characters out of *Blazing Saddles*?"

"I will revise. I told that to the President."

"And exactly what sense of dread do you think derives from some cliché d horse whinnying at a clichéd moon? Get a grip, Konig."

"Just tell me where Emma is."

"To repeat, maybe you might consider resigning from the project?"

"You got to the Ambassador, didn't you? You paid him, and I bet he came pretty cheap. If anything happens to my great-aunt, I'll sue you and the government to the Supreme Court."

"Very noble. The country definitely needs more men who love their great-aunties the way you love yours. Just work, and work well, as you've been contracted to do, or the matter could become serious."

Konig stuck out his foot to trip Kove. Rather deftly, however, and surprisingly, the advisor stepped over it and elbowed Konig just as the President was lapping them for a second time.

"Having fun, boys?" he said. "You're looking better and better, Raymond."

"Thank you, sir."

"So where is she?"

"You can't keep writing your auntie-influenced subversive prose, Konig, and expect to continue to get away with it. Sooner or later I will bring the President around to seeing you for who you really are. Now what are we going to do about it?"

"The way I see it," Konig said, "you've kidnapped my great-aunt and before that spirited away my wife under false circumstances, plied her with phony publication perks, and even supplied her with a CEO-style gigolo—all so I would write this book, which, when I do it in a manner that profoundly pleases the President, you undermine. What kind of presidential advisor does that make you? And, getting back to Emma, you are in really big trouble. If the smallest bone in her body breaks, the fault will all be yours, Mr. Kove. Plus, in slipping the Consul of Brawada several thousand dollars worth of overdue rent to me, you are supporting a foreign government without congressional oversight. Those are serious charges. How would you like to see those charges published, along with *The Midland Kid* and a kidnapping-the-elderly scandal? How would that wash as the President's first big legacy issue?"

"Who's going to believe anything as outrageous as that? Especially as your auntie has a FBI dossier that, I assure you, doesn't contain recipes for chocolate chip cookies and lemon drops. It goes back to handwritten entries and insulting letters personally written to Mr. J. Edgar Hoover, in case you didn't know."

"I've always wanted to get hold of those."

"You do not have clearance, Konig. Long before either you or I was born, she associated with known groups."

"Known for what?"

"Known for really bad things, and please drop the I'm-dumb act. We don't care how *old* a threat to the United States happens to be, a threat's a threat."

"Not from a hundred-year-old lady."

"There's always a first time, Konig."

"You don't have one iota of proof."

"No? Stop thinking about your great-auntie and get to work. And rest assured she will be dealt with, especially if she continues to throw these word bombs that continually are dropping into *The Midland Kid*. You know exactly what I mean, Mr. Konig. Consider yourself and your family lucky so far."

"You're a piece of work, Mr. Kove. Watch out."

"What I am now duly noting is that you are attempting to threaten an officer of the government of the United States, when the only thing you should be doing is ghosting an inspirational and effective legacy western for the President. Is that within your capability? You had better say yes, because here he comes, and he, having delegated to us the solving of our little problem, wants a happy ending. Smile, you little putz."

"Okay, A.B.," said the President, as he maneuvered himself in between Kove and Konig, and they jogged down under the windows of the White House. "As I recollect, A.B., you urged Duke on us as a name for the Kid's horse flesh."

"That's right, Mr. President. I suggested it was a name just right for a pugnacious animal, sir, just like you when need be. As in, Put up your dukes."

"Now, do you remember your objections, Raymond?"

"Mr. President, as always with Konig's materials, I pointed out the media downside. Duke is like baron, like king. It's royal and you know the Kid is a man of the people and he should be riding a horse that connotes something Christian and democratic at the same time, not someone like a duke, born to the purple. The horse should be called Liberty or Freedom is what I advised. I believed that then, and I still do."

"*I* remember, Brewster," said Konig, "that you liked Duke an awful lot. You even began to hum."

A hundred-fifty-watt smile lit up the President's face. "I began to hum 'The Duke of Earl.' Come on, boys, hum along with me again now while we do the next lap here."

With the President doing a credible lead bass line, all three of them began to hum and then sing the emblematic 1960s tune as they passed the portico of the west wing once again:

As I walk through this world,
I know it is my dukedom
Nothing can stop me
Because I'm the D U K E of E A R L

"Nice beat, Mr. President," said Konig.

"Bring it back, A.B. Bring back those good times, those good sessions, and the great prose that resulted. Now why am I doin' this? Answer: To demonstrate a spirit of compromise. Because you remember I was havin' such a good time singin' 'The Duke of Earl' that I asked A.B. if we could have the Kid hum it too as he rides across the territory to hunt down Don Hussein.

"You fought back, Raymond. Sure I was havin' my fun, but you pointed out the obvious, that our hero could not be humming a 1960s hit, fine a tune as it is, while riding his horse in a story set a hundred years before.

"Then A.B. argues back, and what do we end up with? We retained Duke the horse, but we deep-sixed Duke the song. You gettin' all this, boys? Good. I know how to compromise. Now show me you can do the same."

Kove and Konig both nodded. No one was convinced.

"There is something," Konig said after they stopped, and the President commenced a set of post-run stretches as Raymond Kove lay flat on the manicured grass of the Rose Garden trying to repossess his heart and lungs that were, he felt, leaping out of his mouth each time he coughed.

"Yes, A.B.?"

"Well, sir, my great-aunt hasn't received the telegram that was promised."

"Raymond, dead or alive down there on the grass, how come Konig's great-auntie has not received her telegram? Didn't I delegate that matter to you?"

When he did not answer, the President walked over and straddled his advisor. "Raymond, I know there's a lot on your plate, but where's the old lady's telegram? If Konig needs his aunt happy in order to write well, get her her darn telegram."

"It's going through channels, I'm sure it's on the way."

"Is that a wrap?" the President turned to Konig. Half his attention was by now directed toward his wife, who seemed to be summoning him upstairs.

"I'd like you to meet my auntie one day, Mr. President."

"Love to, love to," the President said, as Kove eyed Konig with a withering stare. "But let's get me some thrilling new chapters first. Right, A.B.?"

"You bet, Mr. President. Brewster."

"When this is all over and the country comes to its senses and loves me again, Raymond will arrange a convention, or study group, or some powwow for centenarians. If you'd like, yours can be the keynote old lady. Now, come on. Shake hands."

As Lenore George shouted down for the President from the second floor, Kove and Konig hesitated, and then shook.

Twenty-four

At home, Konig took a hot shower to warm muscles that still ached from his exertion in the Rose Garden. If only he could produce one more knock-out chapter of *The Kid* to make the President say "Wow," and to high-five him as if he had just hit a home run, that, he thought, will give me time to find Emma—and also a reprieve with Anna. Another week or two weeks and she will have the poetry star turn that she seems so desperately to need.

However, as he prowled through his house working in fits and start, the worm of deep self-doubt, which Kove had planted, began to nibble away at his ghostwriter's heart; he came to realize how truly indispensable Emma was.

How had she done it? Where had she come up with such grisly yet wonderfully awful stuff and so well concealed that it made the President deliriously, blindly fond of the prose that thus far even Raymond Kove's most persuasive arguments had fallen on deaf presidential ears?

Vainly Konig went through Emma's room searching for some dog-eared ancient western that might have served as her model, perhaps a discarded Sam Peckinpah film script, a text about Toltec human sacrifice, or perhaps some little-known guidebook to writing western gore, for he was convinced there had to be some printed source he too might tap. He lifted up carefully folded white socks and tiny under shirts and several small lavender sachets. Yet all Konig found in her dresser were an old yellowing copy of an anti-nuclear testing brochure from the 1980s and a photo of a much younger Emma sticking a daffodil in the barrel of a soldier's rifle. On the back of it was written, Pentagon, 1969.

He wrapped himself in a robe, and sat down to work in earnest at the kitchen table. Yet within forty-five minutes, all he could come up with was a blizzard in which both the posse and Don Hussein lose their way, bumping into each other by the end of the chapter. But a blizzard in the Territory? Of course, he could turn the snow into sand, which got him off on the dromedaries that Solomon was still searching for among the dangerous abandoned cavalry outposts, now populated by Don Hussein's sympathizers along the Rio Pequeno. He plugged away several more hours, but when Konig cranked his neck around, he was dismayed to see the wastebasket behind him overflowing, and the floor all around it strewn with yet more crumpled papers. With no Emma, no Anna, and no appearance even by Norman to help or at least inspire him, there was now absolutely nothing to show.

So how was he going to be able to continue to churn out all this stuff that was now due? The revisions on turned-in chapters mounted, the deadlines for new chapters were waiting behind them, and behind them…Konig felt as if an army were arraying itself to go at him and all he had was a dull pencil and empty yellow pad to do combat. He was beginning to panic.

He took out the chessboard, taking first Emma's side of the table, then his own, then he set up a chair for Anna too and began to talk in the voice of each of them. But such mimicry produced only dull mimicry in his next drafts. He changed the Rio Pequeno to the Rio Euphrato, ate half a tuna sandwich, washing it down with a glass of cranberry juice, but it tasted sour. Without the women in the house, little shopping had been done; he poured the rest of juice down the sink and brushed his teeth. Then, on returning to the kitchen, Konig proclaimed sadly to the carton, as he flattened it for recycling, "There are no juices flowing in this house tonight but you, and you taste awful."

He went down three or four times to Paramahansa's apartment, but the Ambassador's place remained completely dark. Was the reception for the Capitol's Brawadan diplomats going on for days, and in an undisclosed location? Surely Kove knew Emma's whereabouts but would not reveal it, and, Konig figured, probably Cheever and Bell did too, but they were out of town once again. Anyway, shouldn't he—at his age and with all those books under his belt—shouldn't he be able to write his way out of this dilemma himself? Yet he never had had a president as a client before, one who may also just be acting the Shakespearean fool at times, but, if so, why? To what end? These seemingly easy victories over the rivalry with Kove, were they what they seemed? Emma said he was being played—was all this part of it? Was he severely underestimating his adversaries?

On the other hand, maybe it all amounted to an important moment of self-revelation for Konig to acknowledge that perhaps Kove was actually right: that a truth had indeed been staring him in the face and for all these years he had refused to accept it. Namely, that he had become like Hardy without Laurel, sandwich meat without bread, a half-baked…he jotted down words, as Anna used to do, but he couldn't even convert the results of this free-association technique to prime the pump of his imagination. Although he now began to fill the pages with descriptions, the attack on Don Hussein's cave was not advanced to any credible degree. Moreover, the fiend's eyes, even in the rewrites, remained crossed, when his aim had been to render them threatening. Nor was he able to figure out the motivation of this new character who suddenly, and, seemingly of her own free will, had popped into the story: the beautiful alabaster-skinned senorita, Immaculata, who entered serving tequila at El Poblito.

Between customers she sat at a lonely candle-lit table and wrote strange poetry, in Spanish, of course. Her favorite nouns and adjectives—tinto, sucre, via, afuera—she spoke them aloud on purpose, so that the vaqueros would think her loco and leave her alone. And they all had, except for Minnesota Joe, who had a strain of the social worker in him along with a growing thing for hot Spanish babes who spouted poetry. The words inspired Immaculata's poetry and reminded her of her ranchero that Don Hussein had burned down in his previous rampage, killing other members of her family. Immaculata went outside. Oh, besa me, she cried out into the desperately dark, coyote-filled night, using some of the beautiful language from Song of Songs, which Abraham had translated for her, at the Kid's request, from the Hebrew, and also words Ibrahim had translated from his well-worn, saddle-bagged Koran. So she wrote in Spanish, besa me con sua boca, but now… Kiss me with your mouth, and I will…

The more Konig force-fed this text, the more Immaculata began to resemble a weirded-out Latina Anna Konig.

In a crisis, hadn't Emma always instructed him to identify the objective conditions of a situation? Look at your own marriage, Konig. Look objectively. So be it. Hadn't Anna left him for oil and poetry? However, maybe the betrayal would be only temporary, especially if Anna knew Emma was in genuine danger. Surely then she would drop everything, even petroleum poetry. Wouldn't she?

Konig searched through Anna's itinerary, which he had squeezed out of Bell, including a few useful hotel contact numbers. He moved Emma's pillows around and eventually came across something else: tucked between the arm rest and cushion of Emma's rocker were pages with press clippings from *The Rig* and *Gusher*, the trade publications that celebrated Anna's latest petroleum poetry triumphs. Up to this very moment, he had refused to read them.

Konig dropped into the chair, removed his glasses, and rubbed the weary cavities at the bridge of his nose. He decided to read "Ode to Spindletop," which had become, so he read in the accompanying article, Ms. Marvell's signature poem, and a big hit at Tonoco's regional shareholders' meetings. There the recitations were often accompanied by cymbals, snare drums, or other instruments crescendo-ing into a kind of gusher poetry and performance piece.

However, the verse was so forced, Konig's writer's heart welled up with pity for his wife's self-delusional career move. Yet was it that different from his own predicament with the *The Midland Kid*? Then Konig noticed a red post-it on the back of the third page, which he had not seen it before; it was addressed to him.

"Dear Mr. Konig," he read: "We're so proud of the fine work your wife is doing and we thank you for 'lending' her to us. Audiences love her recitations, as I'm sure you do too. Anyway, not to worry. I am, of course, taking good care of her. Occasionally I accompany Anna on the cymbals and piano. By the way, what you are writing for our President is also deeply appreciated. Keep up the great work on your project."

It was signed by Tandolea Pryce.

Konig pulled his knees up to his chest and rocked. Days before, while trying to scratch out some descriptive paragraphs about the parched arroyos around El Poblito, he had inferred from fragments of conversations that had filtered down from the twins upstairs that Cheever and Bell had been deployed elsewhere, and that Anna and Lawson Millard were being accompanied by some other officials of the administration. However, it never occurred to him these might include the Secretary of State.

Between the top advisor and the President devoting so much time to him, and now Tandolea Pryce chaperoning Anna on the petro-poetry circuit, were there, Konig wondered, any key officials left in the administration to attend to the rest of the foreign and domestic policy of the United States? No wonder rockets were flying again between Israel and Lebanon, the Iranians were producing nuclear fuel with the ease with which pizzas are baked in New Haven, and the entire Middle East was in the process of meltdown.

Konig fished up the clippings that had slipped to the rug and, with new resolve, braced himself against the chair. Anna's pretty face loomed up surrounded by a frame of Botticelli-esque curly hair dropping down to her shoulders. He re-read her poetry slowly until the idea he was conjuring made itself understood to him.

He positioned the phone and opened the pages to "Oh Spindletop." With cell in hand, like the baton of the conductor, he stood before the window on the parlor floor overlooking Washington, took a deep breath, and dialed. Amazingly, he got through. When she picked up, he did not greet Anna even with a "hello." Certain she would recognize his reading voice, he swallowed hard and, annihilating every note of irony, he declaimed:

> Oh Spindletop, oh Spindletop
> Dug by nigger, kike, and wop
> Oh the hands of enterprise that made you pop
> My beauty, my future, my Spindletop.
>
> Through the storms and driving rain
> And the dark dustbowls of pain
> Strivers from every rank and class
> To Tulsa in their Model T's they came
>
> These not mechanical hordes
> These the People, the Demos
> In their Democratic Fords came unfeigned
> To derrick and rig to toil
> In these dark new fields of grain
> Mariners in Oklahoma's seas of oil

There followed a long silence and then Anna said, "Oh, A.B., that's so beautiful of you." A sense of relief washed over him. Anna seemed genuinely happy to hear from him, a very good start. "I thought you weren't reading any of it. You haven't gotten back to me in days. You know I value your critical response."

"Well—"

"—I'm on a roll, A.B. Maybe you could come out to hear one of these shareholder poetry readings we're doing. They'll surprise you. I do wish you could come, A.B."

The invitation nearly brought tears to Konig's eyes and drove away some of the suspicious noises—were they Lawson Millard's—he was now picking up in the background?

"I'm drowning here, Annie."

"I know you've got big deadlines, working with the President and all. I mean check us out. From nothing to Mr. and Mrs. Literary Power Couple. I just keep pouring out the verses, and Tonoco keeps opening their purses too. Unbelievable."

"I believe it."

"Don't go cynical on me again. Don't you want to hear the other things I'm up to?"

"Sorry. Sure"

"Well, I've got good stuff I'm weaving into the mix, A.B. Oil casts a large poetic net, honey, just like I told you it would. I'm reeling in the associations in *Keroscenes*, which Lawson says they are crashing through to publication just as soon as they can."

"Publication? That is impressive. How is your boyfriend?"

"He's not my boyfriend, A.B. Would you like me to hang up?"

"No, please don't."

"I mean I think you will be proud of me when you see the full manuscript. I've got the Babylonians, and the Fertile Crescent, and the Tigris and Euphrates. I work all that in with the magnificent spotless refineries. I'm evoking the white waters spraying Tonoco's offshore rigs, the noble tenacity of wells pumping away, the sleek confidence of America's jet fighter fleet soaring through the Saudi Arabian nimbus, thanks to Tonoco's new fuel-efficient avgas. A.B.?"

"Yes."

"Are you taking all this in?"

"I am."

"Right. But that's not why you called, is it?"

"No."

"And you didn't call to tell me you loved and supported me…"

"I guess not, although I do. Of course."

"Okay, what's up?

"I need you, Annie. I need you to drop everything. To put aside, temporarily, what you are doing…"

"Now?"

"Annie, how to put this. I'm stuck. I'm blocked. I need you to come home and help me."

"You're blocked on the President's book?"

"Totally. Walled in. Blockaded. An army has surrounded me with orders to let no good words through, on pain of death."

"I thought it was going great guns. Whew, listen to our military metaphors."

"Bad things are happening."

"They told me you were a whiz."

"No longer. It's a real mess. I need you. To help me, to inspire me."

"You're so full of it."

"True, but I also mean it."

"A.B., I'm half way through final proofing on *Keroscenes*. What's your problem? Why can't you just send me the pages? Email. Fax. Wherever we go, there's a traveling office here. I'll be glad to look at your pages. You look at mine. We'll be, finally, a real working literary couple."

"Well, that's just the problem. There are no pages that are any good to send."

"A.B., I am in the middle of a twenty-city tour. New Hampshire, New Mexico, Florida, Ohio. And I have to pack it in?"

He heard a voice in the background urging her to get off the phone. "Who's that? Millard?"

"You must stop this petty jealousy, A.B. That was Tandi. Tandolea Pryce. The Secretary of State. She would like to speak with you."

A voice melodious, polished, very feminine, yet as controlled and sure of itself as a tuning fork, came through. "Mr. Konig," she said, "the President tells me so much about you. I'm Tandolea Pryce, and I assure you your wife is in good hands."

"In that case, Ms. Pryce, could I finish speaking with her?"

"These connubial tête-à-têtes are not what's called for now, Mr. Konig. Anna needs to prepare, and don't you need to be at the computer yourself? There's a time for privacy and a time to work for your president, and now is not the former but the latter. This is not only an election year, it's the legacy year. We need discipline. On message. Remember, you're on the payroll."

"Just five minutes, Ms. Pryce."

"All right. But not too much sweet talk, Mr. Konig. Anna needs to save that for the performances."

"You're using up my time, Ms. Pryce."

"Oh, call me Tandi," she said. "Anna."

When Anna resumed the conversation, she spoke in a whisper and told Konig she was moving to the far side of the room.

"It doesn't sound like you're having such a great time, after all," he said.

"Oh, she's like a stern den mother, but she's okay, A.B. I just don't see how I can come home. Frankly, I don't think they'd let me."

"Anna," he said, "they've got Emma."

"Excuse me?"

"She's off somewhere. She's been away for days. They've abducted her. Taken her somewhere. That's why I can't work."

"Of course you can't. You're upset. How can I work now?"

"Anna, will you come home to help me find her?"

"Two minutes left." Tandi's voice sounded through the telephone.

"I don't get this, A.B."

"It's complicated, but I've looked high and low and I don't have a clue where they've taken her." He told her about the ambassador and the note, but how there the trail had ended. "I bet your handler knows. I bet the Secretary of State knows. Get her to tell you where they're keeping Emma."

"She doesn't make herself available," Anna said, "for that kind of talk. She's all work all the time, and she's after Lawson, if you want to know."

"I didn't," Konig said, "but I'm glad to hear it."

"Why in the world would they bother with Emma?"

When he told her, she said, "If Kove has Emma, and he's not admitting to it, then the President wouldn't know, would he, A.B.? And if the President doesn't know, Tandi won't."

"Anna," he said, "if the President doesn't like the stuff I've been writing, and he's already started not to like it, then—forgive the extended conceit—but there's a good chance *Keroscenes* just might never ignite."

"I know the score, A.B., but honestly, you don't have to bribe me this way. You think I care more about a book than Emma?"

"That's my Annie."

"Like I said, I don't think they know anything about Emma. I've never heard her name mentioned. Anyway, if she's off on some kind of vacation date with the ambassador, what's wrong with that?"

"One minute!" Tandi's voice rang out in the background.

"She's probably having a fine time, A.B. You really can't write without her?"

"She's really amazing," he said with a long sigh. "She's got the whole book figured out—a story line the President loves, but that's not the half of it. There's also a subtext with clues, and suggestions and a style that put him in the grisly light he deserves. Only he doesn't notice. At least not so far. It's a kind of anti-legacy legacy story that only she can carry off. When I reach for the same effects, they're so obvious, they catch me. I mean her ideas are of genius. It makes me believe that she actually did ghostwrite for Emma Lazarus."

"Get a grip, husband."

"Well, that's it. Her powers of invention are extraordinary. One small example. She's convinced the book has to end with Don Hussein's severed head on the top of the Washington Monument. She knows Brewster will love it. Only I have no idea how within the realm of the reasonable I can possible get him out of the arroyo and El Poblito in the New Mexico Territory to be impaled on the Washington Monument."

"Impaled?"

"She was really into it. Impressed even me. Veins swelling, arteries snapped, blood spurting. She was tremendous."

"I don't like the way you use the past tense, A.B. She will turn up."

"Not if Kove has his way. Without her, the book's in danger of self-destructing, but that's, of course, exactly what he wants now. His aim is for the President to forget about the western; then it will be curtains not only for me, but also for you, and for *Keroscenes*."

"You really can't write anything?"

"I keep on trying to copy her magic, but it doesn't work. I especially can't get the gore right, or much of anything else. Emma had a huge knack for gore."

"Time's just about up, you chatty people."

"Oh, all right, all right," Konig heard Anna fending Tandi off and then she came back to him in an urgent whisper, "Don't go maudlin on me, A.B. You can do it. You've written a lot in your life, much of it lousy but pleased the client. This is no different. Find your inner gore, A.B. I know you can do it."

Twenty-five

"You can do it. You can do it," Konig intoned. "Legs out. Buns tight. Pull them in. Push them out. Buns begone. You can do it." Konig was repeating to himself as he labored on his bike to work. "You can do it."

Then as he rode on, nearer to his office, he turned onto a deserted side street and felt it: had the pain not been located deep in his abdomen and risen from there when it hit, he might have thought it a heart attack—which would have been a kind of solution provided it were sufficiently massive. What it was, however, was a painfully deep longing for his wife. Last night, after they'd hung up, he had found the exercise video Anna used to work out and in a gymnastic attempt to get closer to her amidst her absence, he had performed her entire strenuous routine. "Suck it in!" the video had shouted at him. "Suck it in, you can do it, I know you can."

"Suck it in," he now panted as he waited for the green light to change. "Buns begone," he whispered, with a slow soft laugh at himself, and a turn of his long face, as if he were an old horse curiously still stuck in all this car traffic. "Suck it in!" he repeated. "Sure!" and then he rode on in the full knowledge that his mouth was about the only moving part of his body that did not ache.

Although the sit-ups and crunches hadn't miraculously summoned her, they did, however, exhaust him toward sleep. Yet when he had settled in the bed and finally felt the longed-for upper-lid weightiness that might close his eyes, he had heard a noise coming from Paramahansa's apartment, and startled awake once again. Descending in shorts and undershirt, with flashlight in hand to investigate, he surprised a man sifting through the dumpster in front of the building.

Without turning to face him, the man, a large individual in a pom-pomed ski cap, ran off, but not before his retreating pear-like shape reminded Konig of someone familiar. Bell perhaps? No, not him, but Konig could not identify the disappearing body.

There had been no damage, no need to call the cops. The windows to the building seemed fine, the door to the Ambassador's apartment had not been jimmied, and in fact was still securely locked.

Konig had returned to their bedroom, replayed the video for another fifteen minutes—"Suck it in. Push it out. Arms up. You can do it. You can do it!"—and somehow the brief moment of fright and this expenditure of energy had enabled him, finally, to fall asleep.

When he awoke the next morning to the snowy monitor, he felt forming within himself a determination to get to the office and to begin his work. "Suck it in. Push it out."

All right, Konig was now telling himself as he, riding rapidly and with growing confidence, approached the building. He would find his inner Western gore. It just might work.

As he entered and descended his steps, he sensed no Cheever and no Bell, but the paralegal twins were definitely there, photocopying and getting the Mr. Coffee to behave. For a few minutes, he listened to their footsteps and the clinking glassware noises that drifted down. Then Konig settled himself into his chair determined to revise the fire and the flood scenes and to accelerate the confrontation between the Kid and Don Hussein.

He typed out a few lines, which really were not too bad. Suck it in. Burn it off. He worked for a quarter of an hour in intense silence, broken only by an occasional upstairs giggle. Then, however, as his nostrils widened, Konig became aware that the smell he detected was not poorly brewed or harsh coffee. He stood up and sniffed in the strange, acrid aroma that seemed to fill the atmosphere of his basement. No, it was not even bad coffee laced with too much Cremora or one of those sickly-sweet non-dairy substitutes the twins used. What is that smell? Yes, it was less food, more chemical. My god, the thought struck Konig, like an arrow of recognition, in the same instant as the fear: It *was* chemical, an exterminator's chemical, and it was all over the place!

He covered his mouth and nose with a quickly withdrawn red handkerchief and bounded up the steps and found the twins proofreading to each other in the large empty conference room.

"Did you fumigate? Did you fumigate my basement?" Sharon and Sandra stared at him with four bewildered eyes.

"Oh my god," said Sandra. "You're not going to murder us, are you! Don't go postal, Mr. Konig. We beg you."

Removing the handkerchief, he said, "Didn't I specifically say weeks ago never, absolutely never, to fumigate the basement?"

"Oh, Mr. Konig," said Sharon.

"Oh, golly," said Sandra.

"You did?"

"We forgot."

"Oh no."

"It was scheduled, Mr. Konig."

He did not remain to listen. He raced back down, dropped to his hands and knees and ransacked the contents of file boxes and old milk crates. If he damaged drafts of the President's book, so be it; the prose was fairly well damaged already. He knocked over tapes from old interviews, reached around his several bags of plastic knives and forks. He emptied the old bicycle helmet where he stored chopsticks and condiment packets. Sometimes Norman could sniff the duck sauce through the plastic; he preferred it to soy or mustard. For twenty minutes Konig searched frantically, climbing around and behind the hard-to-access stairs and the pipes, calling out the mouse's name as he crawled, but also fearing that any instant he might come upon the creature's limp, DDT-ed three-inch corpse. Still, after examining the entire floor, every cranny and possible hide-out, even after applying his cheek to the grainy carpet in front of the mouse's usual haunts, Konig found no trace of Norman.

His imagination became a matinee of terrifying visions of the creature dragging itself slowly off, coughing, choking, limping to some warm hole in the adjacent boiler room, there only to collapse, terrified and abandoned, and to expire in a lonely death behind a rusty valve. Konig felt like sobbing.

When he looked up, Sharon and Sandra were on the steps descending to him.

"We're so sorry," they said. "Even though we find mice terrifying and disgusting, you must let us help."

The twins insisted on looking once again, but after another half-hour's search, the faint but penetrating poison still lingered in the basement, and yet no body was found.

"Where are you going?" Sharon asked Konig as, silently, like a man already in mourning, he turned off his computer, put on his coat, and stood solemnly at the base of his steps.

"I know you didn't do this out of malice, that you were only following orders and procedures, yet the result is the same: I believe you have killed my mouse."

Sandra caught up to Konig on the stoop outside. She had in her hand some yellow tulips that she'd plucked from the vase on the conference table. "It was a regularly scheduled fumigation," she protested. "You must believe us." With lowered eyes, they handed him the tulips. "We're so sorry."

"Where are you going, Mr. Konig?" Sharon called to him down on the sidewalk. "In case people ask for you."

"They'd better not," he answered with determination, "Tell them I'm going to see the President of the United States."

Then he mounted his bike and pedaled furiously for 1600 Pennsylvania Avenue.

Twenty-six

That evening several helicopters arrived at Camp David, where the President had retreated earlier in the day in order to avoid an anti-war rally scheduled for noon at Lafayette Park. Hearing how distraught his ghostwriter had been when he had arrived shouting and demanding to see him at the White House, Brewster George had ordered his personal physician to give the ghostwriter a mild sedative and to accompany him to the presidential retreat.

Now Konig, still feeling groggy but somewhat relieved, dragged himself into the living room of the lodge, where the President sat watching a football game beside the leaping fire.

Konig noticed, through his tired eyes, that Cheever, Bell, and Raymond Kove were all standing to the left of the fireplace in an agitated huddle, which broke up like a set of billiards when he entered.

"Ah," said the President, "the man we all have been waiting for. Feeling better, A.B.? Have a seat. I want you to know I have complete confidence in your ability to finish our work."

"Thank you, sir."

"Okay. Let's get down to business," the President continued. "Your wife, your great-auntie, and now your mouse, A.B. You allege that we, my, or, rather, our guvment is implicated in all that?"

"Yes, Mr. President."

"I got the order right?"

"You did, sir. I'm afraid my mouse was the absolute last straw."

"Okay, boys," the President said, turning to Cheever, Bell, and Kove, "as you see, A.B. Konig has leveled some pretty serious charges against some of you. These are your boys, aren't they, Raymond?"

"Well, Mr. President, I don't refer to them as 'my boys.'"

"Don't 'well' me, Raymond. Speak up, somebody. I want the truth, and I want it fast."

After a long interval, Bell said timorously, "It's all very upsetting being treated this way, Mr. President."

"They have always despised my mouse, Brewster. I assure you it is a terrible blow to me and to our...our collaboration."

"You see what you boys have done?"

"He's faking, Mr. President," said Kove. "He's acting, as always."

"With all due respect sir," said Cheever, "I concur. It's Oscar Time at Camp David."

"Yes, yes, there will be room for your objections, but for now, just respond to the charge, please. Is it true or isn't it true that you flunkies exterminated my ghostwriter's mouse?" Kove shuffled his feet. Bell and Cheever exchanged a nervous glance, which did not go unnoticed. "I see," said the President. "No one wants to take the fall for the mouse."

"It kept leaving Konig's office and running up Sharon's leg," said Bell.

"It was Sandra's leg, Mr. President," said Cheever. "Sandra's really phobic about puny things running up her leg."

"Who the hell are Sharon and Sandra?" demanded the President.

"Secretaries," said Kove. "Of Cheever and Bell. Twins."

"You want to blame the death of my ghostwriter's mouse on a couple of secretaries. I'll bet they're fine girls."

"No! Not death," Konig interrupted. "Don't use that word. 'Disappearance' is better, Mr. President. You've helped me learn to be more upbeat. Now I'm going really to need it."

"All right, A.B. I'm touched. But you try to get a grip, you hear? What was…I mean what is the little critter's name again?"

"Norman, sir. He's not only my mouse, but my muse. My Norman."

"You hard-hearts hear this? All you have to do is look deep into the man's eyes to see how genuine it is. How broken up this man is. He's mournin' not only his mouse but also his muse. *Our* muse. Essential to our project. No mouse, no muse, no good chapter, no great story, no *Midland Kid*. And the legacy is therefore in grave danger. Do you see the connection, gentlemen!"

"Your legacy, sir, your legacy, sir, your legacy for a mouse!"

"Damn, A.B., that's good. You just think that up despite your grief?"

"Sort of, Mr. President."

"He's ripping off Shakespeare. *Richard the Third*, I believe," said Kove. "The point is that Konig rips off everything. He's a phony."

"I don't want to go there yet, Raymond. Stuff the rivalry. Let's get on the same page here. We can't task A.B. to improve those chapters if we take away his inspiration. Damn. Is the mouse gone or is it retrievable? One of you dead heads, speak up!"

"It was simply part of our effort to make Konig's workplace as perfect as possible for the project, sir," said Cheever. "To help you, Mr. President. To help launch the campaign for your legacy."

"You're not suggestin' you killed the mouse in my name!"

"The man did not have a phone, so we got him one. He did not have a proper window either. How can a man be thinking about your legacy, sir, the long horizons it points to, the future view beyond this terrible but necessary war, if he doesn't even have a window in his spider hole?"

"I do not work in a spider hole. That is a bizarre reference. You see where Cheever's mind is, Mr. President. Legacy's got nothing to do with physical, visual vistas. I like blank walls. The blanker the wall, the better, Mr. President," Konig went on, the words pouring out, leading the meaning, like a runaway train, "because the wall is like the page of the future record and on it my imagination can write our book. I loved my cramped, viewless mess. My office was fine without a window."

"Some beautiful thoughts, A.B., and I thank you for that insight into your creative process. Better get a little more of that into the text, pal. Cheever?"

"So we attended to the window, Mr. President. Then, yes, we re-routed the plumbing above him to make his space more conducive to deep thought, to work with you, Mr. President."

"So, cutting out the crap please, you did or did not exterminate the ghostwriter's mouse?" the President said accusingly.

"It was a regularly scheduled fumigation," said Cheever.

"That's not so," said Konig. "You had never fumigated before. Never."

"Not in your dump," Cheever parried. "But upstairs was regularly scheduled indeed."

"We did not target the man's mouse," added Bell.

"I specifically told them not to fumigate. Never!" Konig said. "What is unclear about 'Never'? They ignored me. Draw your own conclusion, Mr. President."

"We have our employees to think of," said Bell.

"They were disgusted by my mouse. Not afraid of him. Disgust is not identical with fear, Mr. President."

"The twins never once went downstairs into your foul den, Mr. Konig. Draw *your* conclusions from that," Bell retorted. "You're a violent man, Konig. He punched me in the eye, Mr. President. I'd think twice before being taken in by this thespian charade of grief for a rodent."

"Mice are mammals," Konig protested. "Just as we are. And he really was my muse, Mr. President, as I've said."

"Muse," groaned the President. "I just got to be better served by my advisors, Raymond."

"Noted, Mr. President."

"As to liability for the mouse's death, should it be dead," said Cheever, "did you, Mr. Konig, ever put in writing a Do Not Fumigate order? Because I have no recollection of it. Bell?"

"I do not."

"Of course I didn't put it in writing," said Konig.

"Calm down, A.B.," said the President. "I don't put much in written orders either. Heck, and even when I sign something, it's easy enough to change it later."

"Even if you *told* the twins, and not us, there is no written request. Therefore, I'm afraid, the issue of the mouse is moot," said Cheever.

"But they all knew how much I loved Norman. They've heard me talking about him, and to him."

"You *talk* to your mouse?" asked the President.

"Yes, I do, Mr. President. I speak to him in a manner as I would to a pet, like your dog, for example, or a cat. Maybe I speak in a quieter voice because he is very small. But he really knew how to listen. Norman was particularly helpful, for example, when I had to find a way to get Don Hussein's horses stampeded out of the corral behind El Poblito. I took one look at him, and he looked at me, in that sidewise glance of his, and I understood, Mr. President. You remember the mouse we had suddenly dash out near the horses' hooves?"

"A stroke of genius," said the President.

"All Norman," said Konig. "And now he's gone."

"Damn, A.B. I feel your concern, your discomfort, your...but like I tell the generals, even if it seems hopeless, you absolutely got to keep your head up, your body tilted forward a little right into the future. You lean backwards, a sign that you're dwellin' on the past, then you fall on your butt and the whole world is laughin' while it runs right over you."

"I'll try, sir," Konig said. "But it won't be easy, Mr. President. Without my wife, and Emma, and now without the mouse. We had our ways, our routines, and our little understandings."

"You talkin' about your wife or the rodent?"

"The mouse, Mr. President."

"What can you add to the resolution of this little mess, Raymond?"

"Well, maybe, sir—"

"—Maybe what?" the President snapped. "They're your boys, and look what they've done! Fumigate a man's muse!"

"Well, there is another possible scenario."

"What's that?" Konig asked.

Kove took out his clipboard and flipped through several pages. "I've got it here in my research that the pesticide these gentlemen used is not 100% effective. Ants and cockroaches are definite kills, yes, but with rodents and small mammals, the kill rate is somewhat less. It's just possible the mouse survived. It could still be alive, statistically."

"Well that's better'n a poke in the eye," said the President.

"What relief can I expect?" Konig implored. "You've got to do something, Brewster, if there's any chance, any chance at all..."

"Don't we have a mouse retrieval unit somewhere in my guvment?"

"We deal with moles, Mr. President," said Cheever through clenched teeth. "We can render moles inoperable. We can do many things with rats when we find them."

"It's a new world we're in, boys. Think outside the box. If it's a common, normal mouse...what's its name again, A.B.?"

"Norman, Mr. President."

"Maybe just go in the neighborhood. Put up a few signs on lamp posts like you do for a cat or dog. Hell, use my name if you want. Send some agents. If it's smart as you say, A.B., call the thing by its name a few times, and see what happens."

"It likes camembert, Mr. President."

"French, eh? Well, get a load of the stuff and maybe drop chunks around the neighborhood, geniuses! You think you boys can be in touch with Agriculture on this matter? Will that be okay, for starters, Konig?"

"I suppose, Mr. President."

"Go, go go!" said the President with uncharacteristic sharpness to Cheever and Bell. "I think this meetin' is just about over."

Twenty-seven

After the lawyers left, Konig lingered. He, Kove, and the President all sat on the couch before the muted TV and the leaping fire. They were all uncharacteristically quiet.

"Your silence is real deep, A.B., and I sure hope you're not gonna go all Eastern religion on me and have some crazy Buddhists in saffron robes start ridin' into *The Midland Kid*."

Konig, feeling the weight of the presidential hand on his shoulder, bowed slightly forward.

"No plans for that," he said.

Sliding out from the arm, he rose, and said, "Mr. President, sir, if I may." When neither the President nor Kove looked up from the mesmerizing flames, Konig interposed himself between fire and President. He decided to cut to the heart of the matter: "Sir, I've concluded your staff has also abducted my one-hundred-year-old great-aunt."

"Whoa," said Brewster George. "I'm already pullin' out all the stops for the mouse. Now you want me to set the guvment to find your auntie? What do you think, Raymond?"

"We've got our assets deployed pretty well all over the place already. We don't have the resources to be looking for a mouse and an auntie at the same time."

"My concern exactly."

"You don't need resources. Just ask *him*," said Konig, casting an accusing finger at Raymond Kove.

"The ghostwriter's pretty wrought up again. Just when I've been laborin' to bring you two together."

Konig and Kove exchanged a glance that, if sound could be exchanged for sight, would have been a barrage.

"Now what the Sam Hill is going on here? It's about time I knew about everything I don't want to know about. So out with it, the both of you."

"All right, "said Konig, "I believe Kove here personally abducted my great-aunt because he knows I need her to finish our book. He knows I need her just as much as I need Norman, even more so. They're my double inspirations. For all I know he's also fumigated my great-aunt."

"The ghostwriter has lost it. Completely off his rocker, Mr. President."

"Well, what's this then?" Konig said, as he pulled out the note. "I've been studying the handwriting here, and, look, it absolutely is not my tenant Parahamhansa's. It's Raymond Kove's. He wrote the note. Evidence of the abduction!"

"What note is this?" said the President wearily, as he read it held in Konig's unsteady hand. After Konig elaborated, the President said, "That *is* a long time for a centenarian to stay out on a date. What do you say to that, Raymond?"

"I deny it."

"What were you looking for in my dumpster?"

"Now, R.K., are any of these outlandish claims true? Do I look good having one of my closest advisors going through a citizen's garbage?"

"Mr. President! He abducted her, sir, because for weeks now he's known that Emma's been, yes, assisting me to write the chapters you know and love. It's true. I've come completely, totally clean."

"But even so, why, Raymond, would you abduct the man's auntie?"

"That charge is false, Mr. President."

"He abducted her because he's worried she, that is, we, collaborating, will turn out more great material for you. You will enjoy it. It will be a great hit, and the book will lead the way to launch your legacy."

"Oh, wait, wait. I get it, Raymond! You're concerned you won't come along for the ride? Jealous of our ghostwriter-in-residence? You're a silly fella. And damn stupid to do somethin' like this. Hey, as we've always said, *muy casa blanca es su casa blanca*. Where I go, baby, you go. Not to worry. So, where's the old lady?"

"I don't know, Mr. President."

"I'm growing just a bit tetchy and irritated at this evil current that continues to run between you two boys."

"Was that really you the other night prowling around my place, Kove?"

"Raymond," said the President, "zeal is one thing, but…"

"It *was* you!" said Konig. "Where's my aunt? And my wife!"

"All right," said Kove, as he collapsed onto one of the ottomans before the fire, but then slid onto the floor. "I didn't abduct the great-aunt, sir. Not exactly. I arranged for a date is all. Yes, quite a long date to get the old lady the hell out of the picture. However, I have lost track of her."

"Of the old auntie?"

"Yes, Mr. President."

"But, Raymond, your job was never in question. Why in the world?"

"He doubts your judgment, Mr. President. He wants to torpedo you."

"Where's Lenore!" the President suddenly shouted. "This is gettin' too complicated. Wife! I need you."

The President rose from the carpet and slumped into his chair beside the small desk. His fingers began to fiddle with the buttons on the phone. "Gentlemen, what is happenin' here?"

"They're a duo of destruction for your legacy, Mr. President. Make no mistake about that. And to the extent that I'm responsible for attempting to save you from that, please forgive me."

"Oh, get up off the rug, Raymond. Who do you think you're dealin' with here? Nixon?"

"I still don't know where my great-aunt is!" Konig screamed.

"I'm the one that does the yellin' around here, A.B."

"You may fire me at any time, Mr. President, but everything I did, I did out of loyalty to you," said Kove.

"Yes, yes," muttered the President. "Loyalty is fine. Results, however, would be even better."

"If I've done wrong, I repeat *mea culpa*, it's only out of love for you and your legacy...So here's my head, chop it off and toss it in the fire. Disembodied, it'll still sing your praises as it hisses away."

"That's disgusting," said Konig.

"Exactly the kind of stuff the old lady tries to slip into the text to undermine you, Mr. President."

"In all the *mea culpa*s you forgot just one thing," said Konig. "Where's Emma?"

"All right! I'm not unmoved by how you are willing to toss yourself on the ole sword for your president. But, like A.B. says, where *is* the old lady? And what I really do *not* want to hear is that Konig's aunt is in Cuba. I don't like your silence, Raymond. Oh, please don't tell me we have some geriatric wing at Gitmo that I'm not aware of. Say it ain't so, Raymond."

"It ain't so, Mr. President."

"Well, at least I got that for you, A.B."

"That's where she isn't. So, then, where *is* she?"

"They were supposed to stay in the apartment after the reception, the old lady and the Muslim." Kove explained. "When I didn't hear from them, I went to find them. But the place was dark. They were supposed to stay and keep silent and turn the lights out when Konig came knocking. But when I came by, they were gone. Where? No clue."

"And, looking for a lead, in desperation, you threw yourself in the ghostwriter's dumpster?"

"Yes. For the sake of the President, the project, and his legacy."

"Why should anyone believe that?" Konig said

"Because *I* do," replied the President. "Now what is this, A.B., about your writin' and your great-aunt's writin' that I'm missin'?"

Konig was really nonplussed now. He was not expecting this presidential zag after the previous zig.

"Didn't you like the pages I sent over earlier, Mr. President? You said you did. The rewrite of the breakfast-around-the-campfire scene. I replaced all that material having to do with the beans."

"I know, I know," the President said, as he lifted up the telephone, replaced it, and then began fiddling with a manila envelope from the desk top.

Konig observed with mounting consternation how the President grew thoughtful. The brow furrowed, the narrow, if genial, eyes grew narrower into an expression far closer to the public face than the friendly good ole boy visage Konig had beheld during the hours of their writing collaboration. "You made my advisor squirm and nearly cry, A.B. You might be mournin'—and prematurely, I might add—for your mouse and your auntie, but who is Raymond cryin' for? The answer is that he's cryin' for me, and that moves me. Deeply. When's the last time anyone cried for you, A.B.?"

"And I will go to my grave," added Kove, "singing your praises, sir. I'll take a vow of silence. Others, present company not excluded, will try to write exposé books and self-serving tracts. I will never write such a book."

"Oh, shut up," shouted Konig.

"A.B, there's one person I trust above everyone else in matters literary, and I believe I hear her boots clickin' our way right now."

Lenore George entered then wearing the large hoop skirt, white blouse and tasseled vest she favored at the lodge. "What kind of bizarre male bonding is taking place here, Brewster?"

"It just might be *unbondin'*, honey," he said. "Set yourself right down in the chair and read these new pages by A.B." Konig watched warily as he handed her the envelope. "And tell us what you think."

As the First Lady took the pages from her husband's hand, the President stood and began some stretches using the desk as support. Once again Konig experienced that shifting atmospheric feeling of dread. He studied Lenore Brewster's face—growing more darkly troubled as she pored over his prose—and his heart began to beat frantically, as if he were on the last miles of a race he should never have begun.

Twenty-eight

"Oh, Tandi," Anna cried, "I'm so nervous! I just can't go out there to face another petro-audience."

"Of course you can," said the Secretary of State, who was wearing a black pants suit, with sequins running militarily up the legs and arms. A string of pearls set off her long magisterial neck. "I will accompany you, Anna. *Keroscenes* will be a true national hit. There's no looking back. Now buck up, girl."

"I'm not myself today."

"Of course you're not. Who would want to be *that*? Look, dear. Look at you, look at us. Your outfit is fantastic, we complement each other in our looks, our clothes, the way you handle the words and I the keys. Not to worry. Do you want to go over the arpeggio for "Spindletop" once again?"

"No."

"Well, stop looking out from the wings. I've promised that your husband will absolutely not be out in this audience to upset or distract you."

"That's just it. I was kind of hoping he would be here."

"Honestly, Anna. Of course you're a little nervous. You're away from him, and Lawson Millard, one of the energy industry's most eligible, handsome, and richest CEOs, is fawning all over you."

"Not true. I wish you would acknowledge down whose cleavage his eyes regularly stare."

"Cleavage is not a geopolitical term I am comfortable using. Look at it this way. Our blood is running high. We play well, we inspire all those execs out there, including Lawson, of course, and what do they do? They are filled up with…urges. We deny them some more. And they translate their…urges into greater business success, that is, energy production. Because of our performance, we drive them to beat on the heads of OPEC. To explore more, to refine, to ship, to distribute…"

"…I suppose."

"You're not very convincing, dear."

"Tandi, I'll perform if you tell me where Emma Konig is, my husband's great-aunt."

"Oh, no more of this. We have a concert to perform."

"Are you really guarding me?"

"Ms. Anna Konig, I am your accompanist. Listen to them out there. As soon as the earnings-per-share presentation is complete we're on. How can you recite *Keroscenes* and I accompany you with *brio* if we are dissipating our energy mooning about errant husbands and wandering aunties? Concentrate, Anna, and later I'd like to work with you on some anti-Iranian nuclear verse."

"I don't want to seem ungrateful," Anna said as she listlessly moved the pages of the poems she was scheduled to recite, "but—"

"—Then don't," Tandi snapped. "Your frissons of self-doubt will disappear as soon as we step out on stage again. I guarantee it."

"Look, Tandi, there's Lawson. Why don't you?"

"I couldn't, not really."

"Sure you can."

"You really think so?"

Anna noticed the secretary's glance shift once again toward Lawson Millard, who now sent them a short, masculine wave. "It is hard to miss him out there, isn't it?" she said. "He's so tall, so dashing but in that subdued, John Wayne-ish sort of way. Why not go have a chat with him? I promise to compose myself in the meantime."

"Are you certain?"

"Absolutely." With a brush of the fingers honed in her years of waiting tables, Anna now flicked some specks off Tandi's impressive shoulder pad and, in the same deft gesture, removed the secretary's national security earpiece.

"You think it's okay?"

"Go on. Snuggle up. I won't tell."

"Just watch my bag, will you, dear? I'll be back in two seconds. Practice."

As soon as she stepped away, Anna set down *Keroscenes*, and inserted the earpiece. Imitating Tandi's voice was by now easy for her, and she soon was connected with the office of Rick Brainy, the Vice President of the United States. Two or three clever questions later, Anna had the information she needed, and she exited, without further incident, through the rear door of the hall.

Twenty-nine

While Lenore George continued to read his chapter, regularly re-crossing her legs as if to get her bearings on the words before her, Konig stared into the fire, preparing to offer himself—or at minimum his draft—to the accommodating flames. His main thought was to wonder whether he would himself be hoisted right up there on the old-fashioned spit in the Camp David fireplace. Perhaps they would attempt it only later when they returned to Washington. Either way Konig had it figured that the President would soon be cranking the handle and slowly broiling him as the First Lady basted.

Raymond Kove, meanwhile, had gone out to fetch a document, and as soon as he re-entered, the President's wife looked up from his prose. Her eyes seemed filmed over in irritation, as if she had been poring over an open onion.

"How could you, Mr. Konig?" she finally said holding aloft the latest sheaf of pages from *The Midland Kid*. Droplets of sweat began to descend toward Konig's upper lip. "No! Don't speak," she said to him. "I'm not quite finished."

Konig shut his eyes hoping that in the darkness it would all just go away. When, in the next instant, he opened up, Lenore George had risen from her chair and was throwing Konig's chapters down, the pages scattering forlornly across the carpet close to the fire. "Really, Mr. Konig. The preposterous nerve of this!"

"Uh-oh, A.B.," said the President. "Hide your head. She's a-comin' after it."

"Brewster…when I married you, I knew you were not particularly interested in the countries of the world, or their cuisines. I knew your taste did not extend much beyond barbecue. However, how could you—even you—consider this breakfast scene around the campfire anything but an insult to your character, your foreign policy, and to the reputation of our country? I cannot let you put your name on a book like this!"

"I believe it's over, Mr. President," said Kove. "Mrs. George has hit the nail on the head."

"A.B., the work is still subject to some revision, isn't it?"

"Oh, you're dead meat, Konig," said Kove. "You are history."

"You really wrote this?" Lenore said querulously "to advance Brewster's legacy?" Konig stared at her. "But, Mr. Konig, to treat American cowboys this way, Minnesota Joe, and even that Jew and the Muslims?"

"That would be Abraham and Ibrahim," the President said sadly, as if bidding farewell to some of his favorites.

"Yes, but none of them, Brewster, not a one of them could possibly have any idea what a *croque monsieur* is. What kind of a revision is that? And that's only one small detail of many."

"Aw, honey…"

Like the glance of the executioner at the soon-to-be dispatched, the First Lady now turned back to Konig. "How, even by the remotest chance, could these cowboys be sitting around discussing the relative merits of a *croque monsieur* versus a *croque madame*? And even if one of them were this culinary chuck wagon genius, as you unconvincingly suggest, Mr. Konig, still, what is the dramatic point?"

"The only possible point Konig could be making," Kove added as he now stood, "is to embarrass the President regarding the French diplomatic role in the run-up to invasion, because—"

"—Is the whole novel like this?" Lenore interrupted.

"Other sections," said Kove, "have the hints a little more subtly concealed. When Mr. Konig has to produce entirely on his own, without his aunt's cleverly insidious hand, the subterfuge becomes obvious, rises to the surface and becomes plainly offensive, and even ridiculous. That's his dirty little secret, Mr. President. Your ghostwriter has, in turn, required a ghostwriter himself. The great-auntie. But, yes, that's the tone of it, I'm afraid, through and through."

"His aunt? The old lady? The one Brewster sent the telegram to?"

"He *never* sent it," said Konig.

"A hundred-year-old woman really wrote this vile, insulting material?" The First Lady was mystified.

"When I discovered how central the aunt was to this...effort," Kove explained, "I tried to point out to the President several times and he...I had ultimately no choice but to remove the source of the problem from the equation, Mrs. George. On my own initiative."

After he had absorbed this interchange, the President asked, "Despite what you both have just said, I'm gonna direct to my advisor a hard question, Lenore. I'm the President of the United States for another six months and whatever historians of the future say about Iraq, I absolutely know, and I know it now, that they are not gonna treat me kindly if someone uncovers that old ladies are getting abducted on my watch. So, R.K., once again: Did you or did you not, even with the very best motives, send the ghostwriter's great-aunt to Gitmo? "

"I emphatically did not, Mr. President."

"Then where is she?" Konig demanded.

"Say no more" Lenore ordered. Then she whirled on the ghostwriter, "Mr. Konig, the President in his fashion has so admired your past work and look what you've done! It's a trust betrayed. This book absolutely cannot be published. Brewster, do you hear me?"

"But what about our legacy, honey?"

"Brewster, not a sentence, not a word, not a syllable."

"How 'bout a letter or two?"

"You asked me to read the material. Second guess me, if you want, but then you'll have another scandal on your hands, because I'll want a divorce. Very fast."

"That's not good timing, Mr. President," advised Kove.

"I just want my aunt back," repeated Konig. "And my wife. And my mouse."

"Well, I'm afraid it's not that innocent or simple. Look at this, Mr. President." Kove handed the President a brown leather folder in a gesture that conveyed national secrecy and significance. "Shall we show them, Mr. President? Only you can give the okay, sir. Konig obviously doesn't have clearance to see this. Nor, for that matter, does your wife."

"Show them. Show them," said the President after he finished reading. "This is absolutely shocking. A.B., do you have any idea who you have been living with all these years! I'm glad the old lady never got my telegram, and maybe we shoulda sent her to Gitmo after all. You're way out ahead on this one, R.K.," said the President. "Sure, show them."

As Kove held up the folder, they saw a single-page document, which, in large letters at the top, read:

PDB: Presidential Daily Bulletin:
Emma Konig, well-known activist, propagandist. Threat traffic increasing, seeking to ally herself with unsuspect- ing Muslim nation, there to establish base for operations to overthrow our government and way of life. Recommend im- mediate apprehension.

"I'm afraid things will go better with you, Konig, if you help us find your great-aunt," Kove said soberly. "Because she's in a great deal of trouble."

"You've trumped up those charges," said Konig. "There's more fiction in that thing, that PDB, than in all of *The Midland Kid.*"

"I'm afraid you're cooked," said the President.

"She may be a cranky protestor, Mr. President," parried Konig. "Yes, and one with imagination, and, yes, she was happy to try to influence *The Mid- land Kid* with her ideas and her style, yes. But your domestic advisor is far more of a danger to this country than a hundred-year-old woman."

"I wish you wouldn't go there, A.B."

"Is she or is she not associated with one Paramahansa Yogan, consul of Brawada?" Kove demanded.

"Of what?" interjected the President.

"It's a country, Mr. President. An atoll somewhere in the Indian Ocean. A bad tidal location. Sometimes you see it, sometimes you don't. The consul of that country, its diplomatic representative, spent suspicious amounts of time with Emma Konig long before we engaged with Konig here, the great nephew, for the legacy novel project. Although it's been a friendly atoll thus far, pretty much Buddhist, our research also tells us there's a growing radical Muslim minority. Brawada is so poor that with a *jihadi*-leaning cadre, it is potentially ripe for conquest. A violent figure, especially an ancient maternal version such as Konig's great-aunt, could fill the bill. So says our psychological profiling division. She plays well with the local folk religion, she takes over, and we believe she may already have targeted the atoll to set up training bases…well, you know the whole nefarious scenario, Mr. President. A conspiracy requires only two people. It could happen."

"Paramahansa is my tenant! My wife's and my aunt's yoga teacher. A soft-spoken, incredibly peaceful human being. Also extremely short. They are friends is all. Nobody's conspiring except Raymond Kove. He is the one who put them together. *He* wrote that note, Mr. President, to cover that he abducted Emma, and now…he's lost track of them. How could my great-aunt, who can hardly get up five steps, be a danger to the government? All she wants is for your party to lose again in November, sir, and to lose badly, and for your legacy to be mud. And most of the country feels the same way. In the meantime, she also wanted her official centenarian recognition telegram. Is that contradictory? Am I contradictory? Yes and yes. She's a contradictory old lady, not a terrorist as he's painting her."

"Brewster," said Lenore. "Just keep your eye on the main point, which is not this writer's aunt, but the drafts of this dangerous manuscript. Who's in charge of all the working papers, the disks, the copies? All versions of this material, hard copy and electronic, have absolutely got to be confiscated and disposed of."

"Yes, ma'am, I am on the case. That'll settle it, A.B.," said the President. "You won't get all angry with me in public and say things you might regret, for generations to come, will you? Remember the good times we had. Anyway, no one will believe your version of reality."

"Where is Emma, Mr. President?"

"Does the Vice President know about this?" Lenore asked. "Anybody?"

Lenore George watched her husband eye Kove and then Kove eye her husband, and that was sufficient: she knew. "Don't tell me. Really! Neither of you has *any* idea of what has become of this man's great-aunt?"

"Well, as I was trying to explain, Mrs. George: Yes, I detained the old lady, as it were," said Kove, "through some diplomatic contacts. The Brawadan ambassador. Yes."

"And after that?" Lenore said impatiently. "You don't know either, do you, Brewster?"

"No, ma'am," the President said to his wife. "I've been so busy, I delegated."

"So nobody in the government knows where Emma Konig is?"

"So it seems," said Kove. "However, we are working the problem, and I'm certain she's been misplaced only temporarily."

"You will find her, then, won't you, R.K.?" said the President. "Eventually?"

"Oh, the old lady will turn up. We may already have found her. Our people are working all the angles. If she's out there, and especially if the ambassador is with her, we'll find them both. I assure you, sir."

"As a result of my brief association with your office, Mr. President, I've lost, as you know, my wife, my great-aunt, and my mouse. In that order. And they are all still lost. That's a story. I just might write *that*. To hell with you, Mr. Kove!"

"You have quite a temper, A.B. Konig."

"I think I'm going."

"After what you and your aged yet still very dangerous relative have tried to perpetrate on the President's legacy, do you think you can just waltz out of Camp David? After making a threat like that?" said Kove. "Not during wartime you don't."

"Try to stop me."

"Mr. President, shall I get on the horn to the Attorney General?"

"Lord, give me patience," Lenore George called out to the heavens through the rafters of the lodge. "Good day, gentlemen. You've made this bed for yourselves. You lie in it. Remember, Brewster. All copies, all disks, all zips, and the man's computer hard drive as well."

Minutes later, Konig was escorted out of the lodge. It was a sad parting for the ghostwriter from the most notable client of his so-called career. The President didn't shake his hand, and he even asked for the return of the Stetson he had given Konig when they had begun collaborating on *The Midland Kid*.

Thirty

As he jogged down the sidewalk toward his office, Konig feared his errand— to retrieve his laptop and his back-up disks before Kove's men did—would not have a happy ending. For even though they had helicoptered and limoed him back to Washington directly (dropping him unceremoniously behind two old cherry trees at a little frequented corner of the Mall), still he assumed calls had already been made.

When he entered the eerily still foyer, Konig's first glance confirmed evidence of intruders. The coat rack was leaning against a cracked mirror. The side table that usually held the mail neatly on a silver tray, as if it been placed there not by the mailman but a waiter, had been flung to the floor. Dried flowers and their broken vase lay on top of the mail, and most of the envelopes had been ripped open and were strewn across the entire entryway.

Konig certainly expected his own place to have been searched, but why this tossing of the lawyers' domain as well? "Anybody home?"

There was no reply, so Konig stepped in further past the photocopying alcove, into the small conference room. There he found Sharon and Sandra sifting through documents at the large oval table. "Oh, Mr. Konig," said Sandra.

"How come you didn't answer when I called?"

"We're too sad to speak."

"We're moving," said Sharon.

"When?" said Konig.

"Very soon."

"Where?"

"We don't know," they answered him. "It's all very disconcerting."

"Cheever? Bell? Where are the boys?"

"Away, away. Always away."

"And you don't know where?"

In unison they shrugged. When Konig turned to go down to his office, they said, "Be warned. It's a frightening mess, Mr. Konig."

"Who did it?

"You know we're not permitted…"

"Even if we knew. It's all over, Mr. Konig. We're very sorry to say. We've never had such a violent experience before. It's disconcerting."

"Very disconcerting."

"Why do you keep saying that?"

"For people like us it bears repeating. Disconcerting."

"For paralegals, who are supposed to bring about order, to have participated in wreaking its opposite is a very bad development. It gives one pause…Everything's changing so fast, Mr. Konig."

"Tell me about it!"

"We yearn for the days when you were a nobody, and didn't even have a phone." He turned to leave. "They may not be done. They may be coming back sooner than you think."

"But not because we fumigated your mouse."

"Of course, of course. No need to bring that up again. Don't start crying. It was a general fumigation. I understand. You didn't target the mouse. I know. I know."

"How true that is. It's not easy being paralegals."

"I feel you're about to break into a sad song."

"Well, we do chirrup around and *act* happy, but we have been *un*happy paralegals here for some time, and now we're gone. History. Goodbye. C'est la vie. It doesn't somehow seem right."

"What do you mean 'now we're gone'?"

"The men who came, who took your computer, they said the building is going to be closed. Shut down. Maybe even razed and replaced by who knows what. It would be tragic to be replaced by a taco franchise."

"Who were they?"

"That's what's confused us, Mr. Konig. They took boxes not only of your things but Mr. Cheever's and Mr. Bell's. They were large, gruff, and very rude human beings."

"Their manner shocked us," said Sharon.

"It did," said Sandra. "When we said we worked for Mr. Cheever and Mr. Bell, and they had no right to come in here like this and order us around, because they presented no warrant and surely they knew that Mr. Cheever and Mr. Bell are lawyers with powerful connections who would sue the lint out of their socks..."

"That's exactly how we threatened them."

"They did the oddest thing," said Sharon. "When Sandra said that—"

"—They laughed at us."

"It's not easy being laughed at," said Konig, "I can attest to that." Then he sat down between the twins and embraced them, although they didn't seem to be too comforted. "What else did they say?"

"They said...oh, now I forgot what else they said, I'm so upset."

"They said, 'I hope those shysters provided you girls with 401Ks that are very full because you're going to need them. They're history,' they said, and 'this place is coming down.'"

"'This place is coming down'?"

"You can imagine how we felt...oh, can you help us understand this, Mr. Konig? These men, these government types, clearly agent types, were not speaking highly of Mr. Cheever and Mr. Bell. What have you done? What's happened? What have they done?"

"I'm not sure," said Konig, but I have an idea, and frankly, ladies, I think you have an idea too. So why not tell me where my great-aunt is."

"Oh we can't tell you any more than we've already told you. Perhaps we've told you too much already."

"We're so upset. We'll lose our jobs."

"If we haven't lost them already. There is some good news, though, for you, Mr. Konig. Your wife was here looking for you."

"Really! For me?"

"Yes, and she asked us about your great-aunt. Just like you."

"Shows how much you have in common. In our line of work we are delighted to see a happily married couple once in a while. It's a great rarity."

"Where'd she go?"

"We don't know, Mr. Konig. We're not interrogators or detectives. We're unhappy paralegals. She did not offer, and we did not ask. That's our training. But she was clearly a woman on a mission."

"She came looking for me?"

"Of course. But how could we help her? We didn't know, and she came just after that wrecking crew and she went down into your office too. We were dazed. We, who used to notice everything, just sat here, ignorant, feeling foolish, and having a two-box-of-Kleenex cry."

"We did note that she's very sweet, Mr. Konig."

"And pretty too. It's been a long time since we last saw her. We recommend that when all this is over, you try to iron things out. Divorce work was always the least favorite of our responsibilities....Ooh, the things we've been forced to do, Mr. Konig. Perhaps one day you'll write a book about us too."

"Perhaps I will, but first you must tell me where Cheever and Bell are. I know you know because you always do, whether you're unhappy or nearly fired or not. All I'm asking for now is a little information by way of compensation for the mouse."

"We can't, Mr. Konig," said Sandra.

"That would be violating a trust," said Sharon.

"Even if our bosses are bastards who have lost favor with the government, still we're in their employ until we are released. Our sadness for what has been perpetrated against you is great—no wife, no aunt, no mouse, and now no office left either—and please believe us, we would like to help, but a contract is a contract. This is why the heart of a paralegal is often close to breaking. Go home, Mr. Konig.

"Your wife is probably there; in our experience, limited as it might be to legal work, a wife is often found at a home. We enjoyed your presence and your occasional proofreading with us, although you're more careless than we let on so as not to hurt your feelings. Plus your love for the mouse, disgusting as it was, touched us.

"This is by way of saying, once again, go home, Mr. Konig."

"I won't push you," he said, "where you don't want to go, but I have an idea. You don't have to reveal it to me, in so many words. You don't have to violate your relationship with the bastards, technically. Just make it possible, through some signal, for me to find out by myself where your employers are, because there Emma will be too. Deniability preserved. Please."

Sharon and Sandra sighed a sigh that, had it been so directed, might have caused the papers at the far end of the table to flutter. After an interval of silence, he followed the trail of their eyes, which led him, by stages, to the sill of the bay window in the corner of the conference room. There, among memos that Konig read quickly and held up to the twins, was a printout confirming airline tickets for Cheever and Bell to the island of Brawada.

"Is this it?" Konig said.

Sharon nodded and tapped her heart with her hand. Sandra said, "We feel we will never get over your mouse."

"Thank you. Thank you!"

Konig went quickly home. He was not completely surprised to find his building in a shambles too, and the evidence suggested that the same people who had rifled his office had done the job here. Even the door to Paramahansa's apartment had been forced. When Konig went in, this place too had all the furniture overturned, even the meditation pillows had been slashed open and their stuffing ripped out. There was no sign of Emma or Anna anywhere.

Within hours Konig was on the next flight—he was told it would be the last for the foreseeable future—out of National Airport to the island kingdom of Brawada.

Thirty-one

"So you see, sir, we have a little problem on our hands here," Vice President Rick Brainy was saying to the President. "But nothing to sweat, sir. Nothing at all."

Although the bright sun above the flooded island paradise of Brawada beat mercilessly down upon them and the report of a few pistol shots still rang out in the distance, the Vice President's fleshy face revealed not a single drop of sweat.

Indeed, this unique ability not to sweat under any circumstances, *ever*, was one of the chief qualities the Vice President brought to his office, and to the Konig Crisis, which he was now taking in hand. For a president who exercised and perspired as much as Brewster George, Rick Brainy had been an ideal veep choice.

The President, intent on having a swim in the blue waters, as soon as they receded from the service roads around the runway, was looking quite dapper in a brief white Speedo bathing suit and a loose Hawaiian shirt with pineapple design. Now he threw on a robe, offered to him by the Vice President, and sat down to a table with an array of maps to survey the situation from beneath a large white tent several miles from the Brawada International Airport, which had recently been secured by troops of the United States.

"I didn't want to go preemptive again, did I, Rick? But these boobs just forced the presidential hand."

"That's right, sir. But don't you fret. We've got this under complete control. There will not be a hint, a peep, no legacy-damaging leak will ever find its way out of here. Anyway, hardly anyone even knows this place exists. Not even the United Nations. Frankly, Mr. President, this time you made an excellent decision. It's a great country to have invaded."

In the tent, sitting somberly in uncomfortable folding chairs in front of the President, who periodically glared at them, were Cheever and Bell, as well as Tandolea Pryce and Lawson Millard. They were not exactly in prisoner jumpsuits in the physical sense, but they knew they could not move without permission.

"Run it by me again so I get the full perimeters of the problem," said the President. "First, where is the old lady?"

"She and Yogan, that's the consul, Paramahansa Yogan, of Brawada, are at this moment in the presidential palace not far from here," explained the Vice President. "Tandi really blew it. She got a little love-struck at just the wrong time and let the ghostwriter's wife just wander off. The wife's location is at this time unknown, but we're working the problem. The entire army of Brawada is surrounding the palace, but not to worry on that score either, sir, because we estimate the army consists of about twelve boys with a few squirt guns. It'll be over soon."

"Oh sure. We've heard that one before."

"The military aspect is contained. The problem is that by the time we confirmed the location of Konig's great-auntie she had already been here a while, and she was seeking asylum in Brawada and, well, you know, we couldn't abduct her back, so to speak."

"Because?"

"Because it isn't just any old asylum situation, Mr. President. It turns out Yogan is not just the low-level official of his country living on the cheap in the ghostwriter's basement that he represented himself to be; he's the crown prince of Brawada, he's about to marry, and also soon to be king."

"King o' what?"

"King of this kingdom right here, Mr. President. King of Brawada."

"And who's he marryin'?"

"Why, Emma Konig, sir."

"The old lady is going to be queen?"

"That's right, sir. If we allow it."

"At her age? Damn!"

"My thoughts exactly."

"You say 'if.'"

"Well, if we launch a marital preemption, sir, then we can prevent the marriage. This time, sir, you'll be happy to learn that our officers have been quick to learn the tribal ways and now we can put pressure on every justice of the peace in Brawada, so that no one will wed them."

"Aren't I in favor of holy matrimony? Do I really want the opposition to catch me in a policy contradiction this late in the legacy game, Rick?"

"As I say, no one's going to know. But it's your call, Mr. President."

"How far have things gotten, marriage-wise?"

"They had taken out papers right under the eyes of these idiots here," the Vice President pointed at Cheever and Bell, "and the marriage is imminent. As I say, there's the pre-empt on the justices as one option. Under the circumstances, Mr. President, our other options are somewhat limited."

"But I won't sweat it."

"That's why I'm here, sir."

"We could still deport the old lady back to Bulgaria," said Tandolea. "Bulgaria's still part of the coalition."

"That's Ukraine," said the Vice President angrily, "but that is not an option since she's already in the asylum process here as well as in the marriage process."

"Who's she seeking asylum from?"

"From you."

"What did I do to her?"

"Exactly. Not a thing. People make a mess of their lives, and messes all over the world, and then they lay it your doorstep to solve."

"I appreciate the support, Rick."

"Still, we thought you could talk to her. Use your legendary one-on-one, *mano-a-mano* persuasive skills to defuse the whole situation."

"Perhaps Tandi is right and we should just deport the old broad."

"A slight problem there would be that Kove, after you asked him to send Mrs. Konig her one hundredth birthday telegram...uh, we did a little research and discovered she was indeed not even ours to deport."

"Is that confirmed?"

"I'm afraid so, sir."

"Damn," said the President. "Raymond sure lost control of this one. If we'd gotten the telegram out like we shoulda, we'da had time to make her really want to be an American instead of a...what?"

"Brawadan, sir," said the Vice President.

"Go figger," said the President.

"My thoughts exactly," murmured Cheever.

"Mine too," said Bell.

"Who asked you, you unpatriotic, self-serving...hey, words fail me."

"That's unfair," said Bell.

"After you act like freelancers, you opportunistic...words fail me too," said the Vice President.

"Well, they don't me."

"What's your story?" said the President to Tandolea, as he stood, moved back from the table, and began to run in place. "The First Lady is going to be very disappointed not bein' able to play the piano with you any more. Is this any way for State to contribute to the legacy?"

"Hear me out first, Mr. President. If you let me take my heels off, I can jog along the beach with you and we can talk more intimately."

"Stay put, Miss Pryce," said the Vice President. "You and the President's legacy are parting ways. As of now you no longer have clearance to jog with the President."

"All right, all right, people. Let's get organized. First tell me where A.B. is."

"He's circling above us, Mr. President. He made the last commercial flight out of National. We're in contact with the plane. As soon as the waters recede from the runway, we'll let him land. Then we have to decide how to play it. We can bring him right here, or let him go directly to his auntie by the palace, if the gunfire dies down. Either way…"

"I know, I know. Crisis. Who let all those reporters into the terminal?"

"The trip was top-secret, but those pesky writers come by surfboard and inner tube, for all we know."

"But we can handle it. Right, Rick?"

"Can we ever! Absolutely, Mr. President. Like I said, they might be able to report, but who says they can file? But, just in case, let's get the story down accurately, that is, our way. Secretary Pryce?"

"Mr. President," said Tandolea, "I want to apologize. We had no idea these two would just go out on their own."

"We were tired of being messenger boys," said Bell.

"Shut up," Cheever advised him.

"That instruction is applicable to the both of you," said the Vice President.

"Raymond decided, sir," Tandi continued, "that in the interest of getting your legacy novel just right, he could and should persuade the ambassador, Yogan, that is, to, shall we say, occupy the writing time of Emma Konig with other pursuits, which he did admirably. Anna, that is, Mrs. Konig, told me they had been good friends, so it seemed a natural, unobtrusive way to get her out of the picture. A decent plan in my judgment."

"That's the *judgment* of a person who forgot her primary responsibility and lost track of the ghostwriter's wife!" Brainy added, icily.

"Don't sweat it, Rick. Let her finish."

"Anyway, as the old lady was removed as the ghostwriter's ghostwriter, Kove would be able to demonstrate to you, Mr. President, the depth and degree of her dangerous role, and the project would…disappear. Self-destruct. You were so committed to the book as it was progressing, he told me he didn't see another way to proceed. He consulted, and I concurred."

"Yes, yes, yes," said the President. "Then what?"

"Problem was that Cheever and Bell, who eavesdropped on everything, God only knows how, decided, without telling us, to get Auntie Emma

Konig really out of the presidential hair, so to speak, a little more defini-
tively, by flying her and Yogan to Brawada."

"We thought it would please you and Mr. Kove," protested Cheever.
"She would really be removed from the project, Mr. President. Not just for a
few days, but by thousands of miles. We knew Mr. Kove considered the old
lady a mole deep in the heart of the legacy team, and her elimination was
what he really wanted."

"They had no written directive," said Brainy.

"Of course not," said Cheever. "Still a direction was definitely conveyed
in an unwritten, yet completely clear manner, and we followed it."

"Only you see how it upset my ghostwriter!" said the President.

"That's perceptive of you, sir, because there appears to be another motivation here," said the Vice President.

"Don't tell me! Filthy lucre? Darn, first one thing, and then another,"
said the President. "It's always that way in this job. Why can't it be...like
...just one thing at a time!"

"Let me explain, please," said Tandolea, as she rose from her chair again
and tried to approach the President.

"Do not get any closer, Ms. Pryce," the Vice President cautioned.

"Oh, what's it hurt, Rick?"

"Really? If you say so, sir."

"Ah!" cried Tandolea as she kicked off her heels with athletic aplomb
and began to jog in place beside him. "It feels so fine to be running with you
again, Mr. President."

"Well, we do look good together. Want to up the pace?"

"Watch where you're standing, Ms. Pryce. Not too close," said the Vice
President. "Just say what needs saying, Ms. Pryce, and don't take advantage."

"Well," she said, "what motivated them was not, how shall I put it, self-
less service to you, sir."

"I hope you'll let us have our say," said Cheever.

"Don't count on it," said the Vice President. "Ms. Pryce."

"Bell and Cheever knew from documents they had found in Ambassador
Yogan's apartment that Brawada might *appear* to be a poor country and in
fact, by all statistical measures, it is indeed a basket-case of an island. Or was.
Because, in other secret reports, just completed, but unreleased, which they

found—God knows how—there's every indication that Brawada sits on top of a vast new field of undersea oil."

"Crude! Right here?"

"Absolutely, Mr. President," said Brainy. "A field potentially as big as all Texas."

"And it took these bozos to stumble onto it. How come Energy or CIA didn't know? It's that damn intelligence again."

"I'm afraid so, sir. No Brawadan speakers."

"All right, go on, but this is so bewilderin' I'm settin' us a five and a half minute mile. Can you handle that, Tandi, and talk at the same time?"

"Just you watch me," she gasped, but was also high-stepping beside him. "I did get wind of it, Mr. President, through Lawson, Mr. Millard here."

"Stand up, Millard," said Brainy, "but also shut up while you're at it, and take it like a man."

"Yes, sir, he and Tonoco were in league with Cheever and Bell," Tandi went on. "And he kept me occupied, romantically speaking, I'm ashamed to say, so that while my head was turned, I fell on my face."

"That hurts, eh?"

"Yes, it does."

"You were a fool for love, eh, honey?" said the President. "And look at you now!"

"Fool is what I feel, and I'm so grateful to you, sir, for letting me back in to the presidential embrace."

"Sure, sure. But you, you bumblers," cried the President as he pointed at Cheever and Bell, "you two wanted to create a crisis, so that we would have to land the army and preemptively take over this country to protect this great new source. Do I have it right?"

"We thought you would love the idea, Mr. President," said Lawson Millard. He appeared bedraggled, with eyes so bloodshot he hardly looked the petroleum exec he was, but more like Humphrey Bogart having just jiggered the motor in *The African Queen*. "You know the oil business, Mr. President. There's no way we could cut you in directly. Later maybe."

"Mr. President," Cheever quite nearly shouted over the persistent din of distant gunfire, and the noisy splash and spray arising from the Brawadan tides. "The old lady's marriage made this place a clear and present danger, potentially, to our way of life. That's the way we saw it. It's a small place, but the Chinese know about it, and the Russians and French too. So in accordance with the example you set, we struck."

"But you're not the guvment, you numbskulls. I'm the one that does the preempting around here, not you!"

"Well, we had to act fast, with discretion, and there was not a lot of time for consultation. We sounded out Mr. Kove, and then we figured that we apprehend her and, in the process, all this free oil."

"And where does that leave my legacy!"

At the roar of engines overhead, they all looked up, as if with one set of eyes to see the plane, which was identified as the one on which A.B. Konig was a passenger. It seemed to be circling erratically and perilously, as if running out of gas. "And while the whole thing is efficiently done," Cheever could hardly contain his exculpatory enthusiasm, "You, in the meantime, Mr. President, jettison this self-destructive *Midland Kid* project, and...I don't know to this day why you and Raymond Kove do not appreciate our ingenuity and initiative. We maybe read Mr. Kove's mind a little too energetically, but the direction was right. I still believe that. We were operating within the parameters of the clearly designated, if unexpressed, and therefore easily deniable goal. We were being...entrepreneurial. If I may say, Mr. President, we should not be sitting here accused like prisoners in the dock; instead you should be giving us kudos, medals, new licenses to drill, or at least your handshake."

"I'll give you my handshake," said a very irritable Commander-in-Chief, "right across your big lip."

"Let me tie up a few loose ends, Mr. President," said Rick Brainy. "Tandolea has a very good stride and plant, to be sure, but let us remember she also lost control of the ghostwriter's wife. And that was, unfortunately, a considerable part of our leverage to control him and to keep both the ghostwriter and the old lady in the game. Remember we're talking legacy here. These people have to shut it up—long after these events will have unfolded. Isn't that right, Ms. Pryce?"

"To this very minute I'm still not sure how it happened. I never expected a language poet to be so clever."

"Where is the Petroleum Poet now?"

"Whereabouts still unknown, but, as I said, we're working on it," said the Vice President.

"Who is?"

"Raymond."

"Should I be encouraged? Mmm, and the copies, the disks, the hard drives? What about all that?" asked the President. "Lenore says I'm in it deep if we don't account for each and every one. All of 'em."

"Not to worry."

"Not to worry?"

"No, sir. Raymond has assured me. Steps have been taken."

"He's back in our good graces?" asked the President.

"He's always loved you," Tandolea said. "He just...what shall I say...lost his edge because he can't keep up."

"Back to the doghouse with you," said the President, "but thanks for the sprint. Now. Awright," the President went on irritably. "Here's the way I see it: I've got to deal with the ghostwriter and the auntie and this here political crisis and I have to do it on my own...Honestly...where's Raymond and Lenore? Why can't they be here?

"Okay. I've got to emerge from this little tempest in a teapot lookin' really strong. Once we beat the guys with the squirt guns, do we have a plan, Rick? Because all this occupyin', especially a no-count little island, is a legacy-buster, wouldn't you say?"

"Absolutely, Mr. President. But you'll see this will be a real peaceful occupation. I guarantee it."

"More guarantees," the President mumbled.

"In this case, not to worry. Brawada is primarily a Buddhist island," said the Vice President. "They'll remain pretty peaceful, especially if we distribute the moolah equally in both the north and the south. Then, we'll give them all a shipment of brand new meditation pillows to replace the soggy ones; then we drain the runway. It will be a short occupation."

"I don't know about the rest of you people in guvment," said the President, "but maybe there's another approach here. All A.B. Konig wanted was his old auntie back in exchange for our terminatin' the book. If we're destroyin' the drives, disks, and zips, it seems to me we can still cut that deal. Right, Rick?"

"Yes, sir."

"Because as I see it, we put the absolute kibosh on this book, as I say, reluctant though I am to give up kicking Don Hussein's butt and romancin' the hot tamales at El Poblito. Anyway, I still like A.B. in a man-to-man sort of way, and he likes me. I know it, even after all this water has flown down the creek, there's some bond between us and I can get that to ignite again if you know what I mean. But it won't happen with you people crowdin' us."

"You'll go it alone?" asked Tandi.

"I'm fairly certain I can get the ghostwriter to recommit to our deal, but we got to give him back his great-auntie. Because without the auntie it's no deal and he'll go and blab all over the place, and write Lord knows what in his exposé book."

"We can spin and re-spin anything Konig says," said the Vice President. "If there are no records, it's just he said and we said and he's a nobody, this A.B. Konig."

"That's just the attitude I want to avoid. You forget, Rick, that A.B. Konig came this close to being Ghostwriter-in-Residence, at cabinet level. That's how good he was. Or I thought he was. The old lady really wrote all that? Say, I've got it. Have I got it!"

"Got what, Mr. President?" asked Tandi.

"You wait and see. Now get me over to them."

"What about your swim, Mr. President?" said Brainy.

"The ocean will wait," said the President as he strode off. "Right now, after a quick change, I've got a date at the palace."

Thirty-two

The President and Konig arrived from opposite entrances at the Great Gallery of Tides of the Grand Palace of Brawada. They approached each other and the large curving staircase at the very center of the hall, their shoes squeaking across the palace's highly polished floor. The tall young Brawadan guards wore their ceremonial hats of tern feathers and sashes of strung blackback gull beaks, sea grasses, and bright green kelp. Having been alerted, they stood at the base of the stairway, remained very still, and waited.

As the President and his ghostwriter came near, each became aware that the other was wearing quite nearly the same outfit: cross-trainers, faded jeans, white t-shirt, and baseball cap. "I hope," said the President when they shook hands, "that you won't let a little international crisis and a temporarily misplaced great-auntie interfere with our workin' friendship, strained as it might be at the present moment."

"Mr. President, I'm touched you're taking such a personal interest. Let's go see what's up for ourselves."

"No. My administration never barges into a bridal suite. That's private family territory. Let's talk right here."

"Help me understand this, sir. You invade any country you choose, listen in on private citizens' phone calls, imprison people with barely a semblance of due process, and then you're shy of bedrooms?"

"I'm not debatin' you, A.B. And I'm real unhappy about the attitude that seems to be filtering up from those remarks."

"Well, I'm really disappointed in you too, Brewster. And there are about 240 million other Americans who feel the same way."

"You know how to throw a low blow, A.B. Ah, how quickly you've turned against me. Yes, there are millions who don't embrace my message. I know that. That comes with the territory. One day they will be able to listen with their hearts. But you, A.B., you of all people!" exclaimed the President as he stretched out his arm to embrace Konig. The ghostwriter, however, recoiled and back-pedaled, and they continued to talk to each other from some distance, as if from two invisible podiums.

"There's of course been a Judas Iscariot type figure in my political life before, here and there, but after all our fun and collaboratin', I'm shocked. I really am. At this stage of my political life, I never thought you'd be the one to betray me this way."

"People are dying, Mr. President, while you're sending in more troops to no end and worrying about your ego and your legacy. And now this island too."

"I said I wasn't debatin'. Bottom line: you want your great-auntie or not?"

"Yes I do."

"All right then. Let's resolve to stop insultin' each other and get down to it. What she's doin' in the bedroom at her age frankly makes me curious too, in a non-religious sort of way. So go on. After you, Mr. Ghostwriter. I'll follow right behind."

Eyeing each other suspiciously as they ascended, they climbed the grand staircase and arrived at the white-door at the top of the landing, where Konig tapped gently on the frosted glass. There was no answer. "Is the old lady a little hard of hearin'?" asked the President.

"Not the last time I saw her," said Konig. "Maybe because of her ordeal, the way you whisked her away in the middle of the night, you made her a little deaf."

"I want the record to show that we absolutely don't do any whiskin' away or renditionin' one-hundred-year-old ladies no matter what they do."

"Oh no?"

"Don't be such a skeptic, Konig. It don't help your prose. Plus, my administration covers up to 1.5 percent for hearing aids for seniors, by the way, after a $5,000 deductible."

Konig rapped again.

"Come on in," Emma's voice, familiar and yet also different, floated its way out to them. "The latch is up, and the sex is good. We're decent. Don't be shy. People of Brawada, enter."

When the President and Konig did, they beheld an elevated platform, and on it a huge canopied bed. Beneath a comforter of native Brawadan sea-turtle and frigate bird design the diminutive figures of Emma and Paramahansa peeked out.

"Well, Parry, look at who the cat dragged in!"

"Revered landlord! And who's this? No!"

"Yes indeed," said Konig. "Brewster George, President of the United States."

"Howdy do, folks. You're an inspiration to us all."

"What do you want of us?" Paramahansa said. "Mr. President, you should be ashamed. You have invaded paradise."

"Oh, relax, Parry," said Emma. "Ever since we've begun to...you know...mate ...Parry's lost some of his equanimity, but I've gained it."

"Ain't all of life a big fat trade-off?" said the President. "Speaking of which, Ms. Konig, I want to tell you how much I admire the material you ghosted for your nephew here, despite the knife-in-the-back subtext. Did I get that word right, A.B.?"

"Go on, Mr. President."

"All I'm sayin' is that your auntie here has a first-rate career ahead of her doin' hard ridin' men going hell for leather for peace, justice, and the American way. Why not come on home, lie low for a while, and then after November we can fix you all up at yours truly's new presidential library and legacy center after I leave office?"

"Despite the new bliss I'm experiencing, I smell a rat," said Emma.

"We have eliminated the rats in Brawada," said Paramahansa.

"Mmmm," said Emma. "Must be present company."

"Emma," Konig said. "I was so worried about you, I made a deal with the President. He helps find you and gets you back to me safely. In exchange, *The Midland Kid* never happened. We don't publish, we don't talk about it. Nothing. That's it. I'm reluctant to say it, but, yes, the book never happened."

"That's right, Ms. K. Just agree to that and you can go home too, not to the Ukraine or wherever you sneaked in from, but to the good ole USA, and accompanied, I might add, by the greatest army in the world. Keep the money too. No problem."

"Where's it come from, Brewstie?" she said. "A little spare change left over from Halliburton?"

"Whooie," said the President, as he took off his cap and doffed it in Emma's direction. "Gettin' real hot, and unfriendly, in here."

"A.B. and I will not take a nickel of that blood money. Maybe buy a few artificial limbs with it."

"Calm down, Emma," said Konig. "And come home."

"Say, you're a real thrill-seeker, aren't you, Ms. K? If you want I could fly you home in one of our fighters."

"I don't think either of you gentlemen understands," Paramahansa interrupted. "Emma's life has profoundly changed."

"Damn tooting it has," she said.

"My future queen and I are staying right here to perpetuate our love, as is our custom, right before our people, if you don't shoot them all first, Mr. President. Afterwards, we will keep an eye on the new geopolitical situation on Brawada. Namely, our oil."

"Now don't go geopoliticalling me, little guy," said the President.

"Don't you call him 'little guy'," Emma nearly lifted off the bed, from under the ornate comforter. "I happen to be seeking asylum and marriage with this 'little guy,'—"

"—Both of which shall be granted, my love."

"So how about a little respect, Mr. President Brewster George, or in my new position as queen of Brawada, I just might call for an international investigation of your war-making. What do you think of them apples, Brewstie?"

"Bravo, my darling."

"You hear that?" she challenged to Konig.

"You're our darling too. Mine and Anna's."

"Oh yeah?"

"Look, Ms. Konig," said the President, "This new true love you have is a fine thing, but I think you should come home like A.B. says. You got real writin' talent that goes to waste out here in the middle of nowhere. After all our disagreements settle down I'm gonna make more time in my post-November schedule to learn the writin' trade, inspired by A.B. But it's you I want to work with next time, Ms. K., providin' you can tame our subtexts an' all. For example, I got this idea to do a book about the elderly in Florida, say, where they run into big problems because gators are suddenly on the loose…"

"Probably coz of global warming, Brewstie," Emma said. "We don't do something soon, I'm going to lose my new kingdom before I take office. Do something about *that*!"

"The point of the book would be the elderly comin' together, alert and strong as all get-out because they have these private health accounts and their meds are great, so they can take on the gators…"

"All right," said Emma. "The jig is up. I don't help on any such product. Anyway, I'm going to be a queen."

"If you're worried about A.B. here, Ms. K., we can put him on the payroll too, provided you do the prose; he can help out if he's restricted to the spellin' and such. What do you say?"

"Don't you understand a No when you hear it?" said Konig.

"I'm in politics. 'No' carries almost zero meaning for me. But I like that line. Maybe we can get that in our book."

"'Our'? Listen, you pipsqueak of a President, we all know, even A.B. understands by now, that your legacy and your book writing plans have only one purpose: to take attention away from the egg you laid, the worst foreign policy disaster in American history."

"You got a passion for exaggeratin', Ms. K. But I'll forgive you seein' it's part of your gift."

"Just you wait 'til I become queen."

"You think we'll allow that?"

"Oh, Mr. President," said Paramahansa, "it is not to be denied, even by you."

"You tell him, Parry!"

"Just you watch how much denyin'—and a whole lot more—yours truly is capable of," said the President. "Your people really think your sovereign atoll, or whatever this place is, will let you take the reins after we tell them in all their languages what you have been up to for *my* guvment?"

"How wrong you are, Brewster," said Paramahansa. "They will understand. Pressed as my country was, I agreed to work with your most disagreeable Mr. Kove. Even the world's tiniest country must do its tiny best, he urged me, in the war on terror. What a fool I was. But fairly soon my good karma reasserted itself, and my detainee became my fiancée and princess— and queen-to-be. Is that not a beautiful, romantic story! My people love happy endings."

"Well, think hard on it, king, or prince, or whoever you are. She's got a lot of miles on the ole odometer too."

"If you'd gotten your government together to give me my telegram, maybe things would have been different. But I doubt it, you oil profiteer you!"

"Say, you are one tough old lady," said the President. "Listen, if I cook up somethin' telegram-wise in the next few minutes, would you play ball? Anyone got a cell phone?"

"Too late, Brewstie, you election-thief you. You war-monger, you. Soon the marriage ceremony, and then I will be—what's my title, Parry?"

"Turtle Queen of Brawada."

"A head of state, and your equal, pal."

"Kinda cute," said the President.

"You're not even invited to the coronation, Brewstie. Don't let him come, A.B. Get the army out of this peaceful paradise while you're at it."

"I'm your closest living relative, Emma. I thought you might at least have consulted me before you decided to marry."

"Let me see a smile, A.B. Soon I'm going to be—the Turtle Queen." In a gesture Konig had never seen, and which she had obviously learned on the atoll, Emma lifted her hands up regally above the comforter. "This is the way I am going to bless our people, Brewstie, just as soon as you get the Marines the hell off my island."

"I'll wait to hear what the commanders on the atoll tell me."

"Well, I'm telling you and Parry is too. Remove the troops, so we can practice our wedding."

"You're kidding," said Konig.

"Am I? I don't think so. I'm going to marry and you should publish the book, A.B. So the deal's off, Brewstie. "

"But, Emma," said Konig, "considering who you are, your background, how can you become a queen and start lording it over people, even the turtle people?"

"Say it like it is," the President said, with a nod of approval to his former ghostwriter.

"Tell 'em, Parry."

"Revered Emma will, it is true, be queen to my king, should our beloved and very aged king perish soon, which, alas, seems likely. Yet here, in our country, life is so fragile, with the tides and the undertow, and the inability to support ourselves, well, as a result, Brawadans, as long as they live, refer to each other as 'king' and 'queen.' Every husband is a king to his wife, and every wife a queen to him."

"It's a royal democracy, and my kind of place."

"Still, look at it realistically, Ms. K." said the President."

"Would you mind calling me your highness, Brewstie? So I can get used to it."

"Whoa! You're a hundred years old and counting, Ms. K. You're in bed with this little king who's maybe what? Four foot tall. On a sinking island that is occupied by the troops of the most powerful nation on earth—America, God bless her. I'm maybe not the brightest president there ever was, but I'd say I've got quite an advantage here."

"When one party acts out of love," said Paramahansa, "and the other out of greed for oil, who will prevail?"

"Well, can't let it happen," said the President. "Ms. Emma Konig, if you in fact do become a head of state, that just might present a danger to us, a threat, especially given your past pronouncements. And there is no threat I don't squash preemptively, even from old ladies and islands in the middle of nowhere. Even though my people tell me nobody's heard of the place, it could still be a launching pad, a platform. And in my book a platform that's half under water is still a platform, still a potential political danger. You understand, don't you, A.B.?"

Konig was silent. He looked at his Emma and at the President.

"In Brawada," said Paramahansa, "we always avoid waves. On the other hand, we already have had a few outspoken queens. You, darling, will be in that tradition."

"You've already got the army here, Mr. President," Konig said. "And I saw reporters all over the place. You've got a lot of explaining to do regardless of whether Emma becomes queen."

"Don't kid yourself, A.B. I only seem inept. If I want to, I know how to instruct my people to shut this little atoll down lickety-split; impose a blockade; quarantine, guillotine everything that moves—the works. Keep every reporter eating out of my hand, so that the invasion, so-called, as well as *The Midland Kid*, will not have happened. No one will ever know about either of them for all recorded time, or, more importantly, at least not until the legacy is out there percolatin' among the people. Your only choice, Ms. Emma, will be which country we deport you to, citizen or not—to Bulgaria or the Ukraine. Believe me, we can deport first, and they can ask questions later."

Emma sat bolt upright in bed. "Speak truth to power, sonny," she said to Konig. "Tell this sonuva…tell this poor excuse of a president I will marry who I want, be queen of whatever atoll I choose, and you will publish what you want, provided you can find some damn fool publisher to do it for you. And, in the process, send this man's legacy where it deserves to be—at the bottom of the list along with Fillmore, Polk, Hays, and all the rest of those strike-breakers!"

"Who?" said the President.

"Calm yourself, my queen,' said Paramahansa. "In the Brawadan spirit of compromise, it is possible we can marry here, and also return to live in your lovely dwelling in D.C., as in days gone by? I occasionally grow weary of the sea and long for my basement in the City. We can be king and queen of Brawada in loving absentia, and the world needn't know and needn't bother with us. Is that an option for us to discuss later, so as to put the kibosh on the loneliness for you that your great-nephew might experience? Yes. However, as a sovereign leader, just like you, I say, no way to this president. Therefore, Mr. President, withdraw your army, and leave Brawadan oil for Brawadans."

Emma threw her arms around her prince, kissed his bald dome, and then ran her fingers down the sides of his head, and tickled his ears. "He's short, but he's a real man."

"What's with the earlobes?" asked the President.

"Brawadan custom," said Paramahansa. "The earlobe is one of the parts of the body that never ages. The lobe is revered by our people."

"Well, that's very touching," said the President, "but you people can't spend all your time at nookie and playing with your earlobes and hope to have any kind of energy infrastructure here. Your oil's doin' you no good. Your international airport is good for nothin' but ducks and water polo. You need us because with your chopsticks or whatever it is you use over here, you can't get within three football fields of that oil. That's why our boys are here already. To help, to serve, and to drill."

"Perhaps we will leave it in the ground," said Paramahansa, "so that life will go on here, as always: flooding, drying out, flowering, and flooding once again. The impermanence inherent in nature."

"I will do anything my great-aunt wants," Konig pronounced.

"Publish the book," Emma said, "and sink this man's boat."

"Well, he can't, Ms. K., because all the disks and the computer are gone. Disappeared. Poof!"

"You do remember, Mr. President," said Konig, "that you promised I could write a book about the writing of the book?"

"I remember, A.B., but I also said I would do everything in my power to give you a hard time, and I will. Starting now. I mean I already have. A.B. knows already that he has got no computer record of the book, no disk, *bobkes*, as you writers say. Right, A.B.?"

"I'll show you *bobkes*, Mr. President. Parry, may I borrow your cell phone?"

"Of course, my queen."

Emma took Paramahansa's cell phone, deftly flipped it open, and placed a call.

"Reception's a little difficult at high tide," said Paramahansa, "and when the enemy air force is circling overhead."

"I'm impressed," said Konig to Emma. "You not only discovered love; even more useful, you've learned how to operate a cell phone."

"Yup, and guess who I'm calling."

"Careful," said Paramahansa, "they are probably listening in."

"My guys?" said the President. "I should be so lucky."

In an instant Emma was saying hello and passing the phone to Konig. "Who is this?"

"*Your* queen," said Paramahansa.

"Anna?"

"Come on. This is really rude. I'm the President."

Yet the President watched and listened as the muscles of Konig's face, which had not formed themselves into such a wide smile in many weeks of his writing ordeal, now discovered they still knew how. His cheeks rose and pulled up the ends of his mouth, and a half circle of pleasurable amazement formed with his lips.

"You're kidding? You are the most wonderful person in the world." Konig listened for several more minutes while Emma and the Ambassador snuggled and the President squirmed and paced about the bridal suite. "I can't thank you enough, and I can't wait to see you!"

"All right," said Emma. "This island is becoming lousy with love. Us, and now my great-nephew here and his wife. That leaves you, big boy. If you want to be in touch with your honey, Mr. President, I've got a great calling plan. Dial away."

"Out with it, A.B. Who was that on the phone? Is there somethin' specific I have to fear, based on your newfound happiness, or is it only fear itself?"

"Really great news."

"Tell him," said Emma.

"That was my wife. She got to my office and…you thought all the disks were taken care of, didn't you, Mr. President?"

"Uh-oh." Brewster George nearly fell onto the bridal bed. Emma and Paramahansa made room for him, and they began to stroke the presidential earlobes.

"Cut that out, you two."

"My wonderful Anna," Konig said, "got to the office in time, before…she found a disk with most of our work intact, Mr. President. *The Midland Kid* rides."

"Our boys are certainly doing a fine job lately. How did that happen? Who leaked?"

"The disk was in its plastic envelope, and the envelope was in a small box that had apparently fallen behind the desk. It eluded your searchers, Mr. President. And guess what else was in the box?"

"Let me guess," said the President. "Your mouse."

"Yes! Bingo! The disk was a little nibbled, but he doesn't go for that kind of thing. Norman saved the disk, and *The Midland Kid*."

"A mouse, a mouse," said Brewster George glumly, from the bridal bed, where a sudden weakness he hadn't experienced beforehand compelled him to refrain from exercise. Uncharacteristically he kept sitting, and repeating "My legacy for a mouse. Who said that?"

"You did," said Konig.

"I think I'll take you up on that phone call," he replied.

While the President tried to get through to the White House and his wife, Emma, Konig, and Paramahansa chattered away. The plans for the wedding in Brawada would be simple, and the new king and queen would indeed split their time between their paradisiacal atoll and Washington, D.C.

For his part, the ghostwriter, once more, was going to rethink his career, but Anna Konig had said she was definitely going to get back to her verse.

ABOUT THE AUTHOR

Born in Chicago in 1946 and raised in Los Angeles, Allan Appel is a novelist, poet, and playwright whose books include *Club Revelation*, *High Holiday Sutra*, winner of a Barnes and Noble Discover Great New Writers Award, and *The Rabbi of Casino Boulevard*, a finalist for the National Jewish Book Award. His writing has appeared in *The National Jewish Monthly*, *The Progressive*, and *National Lampoon*, and his plays have been produced in New York, Chicago, New Haven, and Provincetown. He has published six novels, a biography, two collections of poetry, a book on botany, and *A Portable Apocalypse*, a handy anthology of erudite and humorous quotations about the end of the world. Among his plays, *Dear Heartsey*, a staged adaptation of the letters of a colonial New Yorker, Abigail Franks, was commissioned by the American Jewish Historical Society, and was presented, starring Anne Jackson and Eli Wallach, at the Jewish Museum in New York, at Queens College, City University of New York, and at Yale University.

Allan Appel holds degrees in writing and comparative literature from Columbia University and City University of New York, and he attended the Jewish Theological Seminary of America. He has taught writing and literature in the New York City schools, at the City University of New York, and at Upsala College in New Jersey. He has worked extensively as a writer for non-profit cultural institutions, including The New York Public Library, The American School for Classical Studies at Athens, and The American Museum of Natural History. He has been Director of Institutional & Foundation Giving at the Museum of Jewish Heritage—A Living Memorial to the Holocaust in New York City. A reporter with *The New Haven Independent*, he lives in New Haven, Connecticut, and in 2003 and 2007 was awarded fellowships in fiction from the State of Connecticut Commission on Culture and Tourism.

1735246